Maureen Hughes has made Law Enforcement a career. Currently, she investigates various crimes as a private investigator. Best known for solving a 56-year-old cold case. She has authored four True Crime books. She has written for the Saint Louis Post, and numerous magazines. She shares her time in Nevada and Illinois.

My deep appreciation to the lady who shared her story of survival in a death camp during WWII with me. And as always, to my family and friends who have said, Bravo!

Maureen Hughes

THE SKIN GAME

Taken From A True Story

AUSTIN MACAULEY PUBLISHERS™
LONDON • CAMBRIDGE • NEW YORK • SHARJAH

This is a work of fiction. Names, characters, businesses, places, events, locales, and incidents are either the products of the author's imagination or used in a fictitious manner. Any resemblance to actual persons, living or dead, or actual events is purely coincidental.

Ordering Information
Quantity sales: Special discounts are available on quantity purchases by corporations, associations, and others. For details, contact the publisher at the address below.

Publisher's Cataloging-in-Publication data
Hughes, Maureen
The Skin Game

ISBN 9798889108290 (Paperback)
ISBN 9798889108306 (ePub e-book)

Library of Congress Control Number: 2023922420

www.austinmacauley.com/us

First Published 2024
Austin Macauley Publishers LLC
40 Wall Street, 33rd Floor, Suite 3302
New York, NY 10005
USA

mail-usa@austinmacauley.com
+1 (646) 5125767

1

Another homicide was reported by Chicago police this morning. Around 3:20 a.m., the body of an elderly man was found in an alley off Michigan Avenue, with the same grisly characteristics of the unsolved murder two months ago in Chicago. At this time, the police declined to give further details. This is Kate Watson reporting from WBCS; and now, the weather.

Detective Samantha O'Malley was oblivious to the radio as she sat at her desk and stared at the open folder containing the Gold Coast homicide case she had worked on for three weeks. With a minor in WWII history, she felt there was a strong connection between the hideous acts committed by the Nazis in 1943 and the case she was working on now.

The tall, slender, blonde, thirty-five-year-old detective, who had modeled for Marshal Field's and Neiman Marcus department stores to pay for college, knew she was missing something or someone in solving the case. She was well known in police circles and the public through newspapers and other media for solving cases the Chicago police couldn't.

She had a reputation for catching the villain by going by the letter of the law and bending the rules only when necessary. That time, Chicago was shocked when a successful, elderly jewelry businessman had been murdered outside of his store. The circumstance of the death had been extremely unusual and little evidence left behind at the scene.

It was early Saturday morning. The grandfather clock struck 6 a.m. She shut the computer down and rubbed her eyes. She needed a break from the murder case reports. Snow floated by her window as the radiator behind her popped and crackled as if ready to give up the ghost.

Winter was not giving up even though it was early April. The chill in the office forced Samantha to pull the cable knit sweater from the back of her chair over her shoulders. She reached for the mug of coffee by her typewriter, but it too was cold, and she decided to leave it there.

As she gathered her notes and folders together, she heard the familiar door chimes ring, indicating someone was coming into the reception area of her business.

"Mornin', Sam! Did ya' catch the news?"

She looked across the office to see her part-time detective, Mitch Gillini, standing in the doorway. Mitch was always meticulously groomed, wearing his signature black turtleneck sweater, leather jacket, and blue jeans. He was all of six feet five inches, 210 lbs., mostly muscle, with a Greek god sculptured face, all beautifully put together by a woman's standards.

He had a dry sense of humor and the unique ability for knowing who the guilty person was.

Holding two Styrofoam cups of steaming coffee from White Hen Pantry, he kicked the door closed behind him.

"What news? Whatever it is it better be good news. I've spent all night with bad." Sam reached for the hot brew.

"Another body found on Michigan Ave. This time in the alley by Kramer's Men's Wear."

"Was it Otto Kramer?"

"I'd say so from what was left. No skin on the upper and lower torso. Everything was just like the Miller case. Nothing removed but his coat, gloves, shirt, shoes and…and skin. The clothing was in a pile next to him along with his watch and ring. The ring has a diamond in it…and wasn't taken. Heck, Sam, his hair wasn't even messed up!"

"Who found him?" She asked, standing up and leaning closer to the crackling register.

"Sergeant Mueller and her partner, Officer Morton, responded to the 911 call. A sanitation department driver saw a body in the alley and called the police. Both officers have been on the midnight shift for eons, and I hope the captain leaves them there! I've seen them together in the park."

Samantha smiled at Mitch. The two cops had a romantic relationship outside of work and Mitch had no acceptance of Mueller's sexual preference.

"Drink the coffee while it's hot," Mitch said as he walked to the window and lit a cigarette. The wind was still blowing, and flurries collected on the window.

Samantha took a sip of the coffee and locked her desk. Shuffling the papers and police reports, she shoved them in her briefcase.

"No smoking in here, Mitch."

"Yeah, I know." He continued smoking, seemingly deep in thought.

Grabbing her coat, briefcase, and coffee, she headed for the office door. She gave Mitch her customary 'I'm not going through until you move' look. Mitch, grinning, stepped aside so she could exit the doorway without being accosted and closed the door behind him.

Mitch Gillini grew up two doors down from the O'Malley family. He was the ten-year-old kid that soaped everyone's car windows on her side of the street every Halloween. The guy who walked her to school every day until they graduated from high school. The same young man who was protective of her at the police academy and swore his undying love for her the day she graduated.

It was touching, as she had no clue, he had feelings for her in that way. It only worsened matters when she told him she wasn't in the market for a romance but wanted a career in law enforcement and to concentrate solely on that. Her grandfather, father, and uncle, all served Chicago as police officers and that meant big shoes to fill.

"Keep up with me. I'm hungry and you're buying," Samantha said as they left the building and faced the bitter Chicago wind.

"My car is parked at the corner. We'll take it." She dreaded hearing 'my car', wishing she had suggested she drive first but said nothing.

"My God, Mitch! Don't you ever clean this thing you call a car?" Pushing the food wrappers and ashes off the car seat and stacking the cups with moldy coffee remains in the cup holder, she squeezed in. "By the way…when are you going to pay those parking tickets under the wiper blades?"

"I have two theories on that. I figured you could get some of them off my record by saying we were on a case or in court. The other tickets I could leave where they are, and the meter maid will assume I've already been ticketed and walk on by. Pretty clever huh?"

Mitch always had reasons that were only valid to him for every misdemeanor he ever committed. He could be a pain in the neck and other body parts, but Samantha wouldn't want anyone else as a partner. She had served the city for fifteen years in the police department and Mitch was going on eighteen. She had passed every test there was with high scores but was passed over when the hiring took place.

She didn't even come in second. Her life was moving on, but she wasn't moving up...at least not within the police department. She took her two weeks' vacation and decided to turn in her badge when she returned. With a master's in criminal justice and a newly minted private detective license, she had decided to start her own investigation business.

Mitch stayed with the department, wanting to retire, and worked for her on the side.

"Let's eat at Mike's on Rush Street," Mitch suggested, hopefully changing a subject he wasn't going to win. "I like the omelets there." Mitch maneuvered the six-year-old Chevy in the slush tracks that vehicles had made in the snow that fell overnight. The sun was bound to shine soon, so the slush would not last long. After all, it was April.

Mike's was crowded with early morning coffee drinkers and the previous night shift gossip.

Mike Morrison's father, Paddy, had started the 'cop stop' in the early 60s and it had become a regular place for cops working all shifts. The business started serving only breakfast and lunch but post-war veterans who couldn't sleep and vets that became cops when they came home used it for a hangout. Business boomed, and two more shifts were added, making it an all-night restaurant.

Paddy Morrison was a typical Irishman with a smooth gift of gab and a sharp sense of humor.

An amateur boxer, Paddy settled down and bought an old café when Marge, his wife, became pregnant. The morning that Paddy announced the birth of his son, everyone received a free breakfast. Paddy even changed the café's name to Mike's in his first son's honor.

For a while, war stories were left to the guys at the far end of the bar to talk of their time on the front in Japan. By the time Mike started high school, the business was paid for and a small addition was added. Paddy had visions of Mike taking an interest in the place and eventually taking over the business when Paddy retired.

But Mike had seen enough badges and had heard enough stories, if only one side of them, that he knew what line of work he would go into. Upon graduation from the Chicago Police Academy on Maxwell Street, Mike was given his own badge to wear. Paddy Morrison's kid had made him proud. And his disappointment of his son not taking the business over soon left. He realized this was what his son wanted.

Beyond the glass and metal door of the café, eight worn vinyl-covered bar stools lined the customer side of the counter. It was understood that the stools were reserved for designated officers and when an officer was on vacation or sick, the stool remained unused. Six booths and eleven small tables filled the rest of the floor space. No signed photographs of movie stars or popular politicians hung on the walls.

Just framed pictures of high school and little league sports teams that the CPD and Mike's café had sponsored over the years, and officers who had died in the line of duty, plus a faded close-up of Paddy in a Los Angeles boxing ring. A large black vent hood hung over the grill behind the counter. The continuous hum of the vent competed with the sizzling sound of bacon and burgers.

Raucous sounds came from all four corners as cops retold stories of the night before. Dishes clamored on the counter as Paddy slid breakfast plates with greasy eggs over easy, two sausage patties and buttered toast to the end of the counter. Nelli and CeCe, the morning waitresses, filled coffee mugs and yelled orders to Paddy.

This was the sixty minutes the guardians of the night rehashed their tales. It was here that they tried to leave the violence and ugliness of the streets in the bottom of their coffee mugs before going to the more peaceful part of their life called home and, "Hey, Mitch, are you ordering ribs rare for breakfast?" Officer Levi Kanter shouted out when he saw Mitch and Samantha enter the café.

"Shut up, Levi. You're a sick pup and butt-ugly to boot!" Mitch shouted back.

The men at the counter turned to Mitch and laughter filled the room. Samantha slid across the hard-plastic booth seat of the corner booth. Mitch followed with Nelli at his heels carrying two cups of coffee.

"Good morning, Detectives! What will it be today? Canadian bacon and omelets are the special."

"The ham omelet will be fine for me…just nothing raw!" Mitch said.

"And for you, sweetie? The usual?"

"Sure but add a banana," Samantha confirmed, stirring her coffee.

"So, what did Mueller and Morton have to tell you about the murder?" Samantha asked when Nelli disappeared into the kitchen.

"I only spoke with Levi Kanter. He was backup. Mueller and Morton were already off shift. Kanter stayed behind for some reason. I talked with him while the police photographer was taking the pics. Most disgusting thing. The bastard that is doing this is meticulously removing the skin and apparently taking it with him."

"The flesh is exposed, the nipples are left intact and, strangely, little blood evidence is left at the scene. I reckon the cold weather is preventing the blood from running."

"Who called it in?"

"Truck driver from the sanitation department," Mitch said between bites of toast.

"Did the driver say anything?"

"Dispatcher only said he was shook up at the sight."

"We want to talk with him. Does Levi think Kramer was killed somewhere else and the body moved to the alley?" Samantha asked.

"He doesn't think so, but he's waiting on the pictures to be developed and the autopsy report. With no blood on the ground, it's hard to say, but I think he was killed and the skin removed postmortem right where he was found."

"Here ya' go. Hot off the grill." Nelli placed the steaming plate in front of Mitch. "And for you a bowl of cornflakes, a banana, and a tall milk. Enjoy and eat all of it...you both look like Hell!" Nelli smiled and let them eat in silence.

"Um...by the way, the chief wants you to call him Monday," Mitch said. "You know he's going to want you on the case. You solved the Lake Shore Drive murders two years ago when his own people couldn't, and the family members hired you. This is the second body in, what, a couple of months? He'll be asking for your—"

Slapping her spoon hard on the table Samantha said, "Did you forget I left the department because the captain didn't see any advancement for me within the department but always wanted me on investigations that his own detectives couldn't solve? Chief Van Watson always supports the captain's decisions. The captain sees only one purpose for me until his dick is in a wringer! I've seen the way he looks at me."

Raising her voice, she continued. "As for good looks...blame my parents. As for intelligence...I've earned everything I have with hard work! I've proven myself in every case I took. I'm very good at what I do, and he can't handle that! Does the captain and his puppets think that my independence and success is due to sleeping around?"

Samantha was cut off by a round of applause erupting in the café. The other officers had turned to hear her and shouted, "Way to go, Samantha!"

"Sure, I'll call him. And I'll remind him that I have my own investigation business and people. And when I tell him my price, I guarantee it will be a short conversation!"

"Okay, okay, I just wanted to give you a heads-up," Mitch said as he pushed uneaten remnants of his omelet aside. “The Tribune is all over these murders and the department, Sam. The chief doesn’t need bad press. Election being eighteen months away…people remember this stuff. The city machine wants results…positive results.”

Mitch, seeing that breakfast was definitely over, picked up the check as Samantha, not wanting to continue the subject, had gathered her coat and gloves, and scooted out of the booth.

“What next boss…the coroner’s suite?” Together they walked out of Mike’s and squinted in the early morning sunshine.

“Mitch, see if you can discreetly get a copy of the Kramer report at headquarters. I’ll take it home with me over the weekend. There were two vehicular fatalities and one supposed suicide between yesterday early morning and midnight. Even though this homicide is a priority, Dr. Cullen won’t start the autopsy on Kramer until Monday morning anyway.”

Snow had melted leaving the streets with puddles of muddy water on the way back to the office. Samantha waved to Mitch as his car sputtered away from the curb. The bitter Chicago wind rattled her business sign that hung from an ornate wrought iron post at the end of the sidewalk that led to her building. Tree branches bowed, but blossom buds were starting to show the first hints of spring.

Three years earlier, Samantha learned of her parents’ death in a phone call. The fifty-year wedding anniversary trip to Mexico ended when their plane crashed with no survivors. Their death changed the way she thought about her future. Her own mortality became her focus, and she needed to re-think her life.

With Mitch's encouragement, she followed her dream of starting her own criminal investigation business. She used her inheritance to purchase an old building on Oak Street. The prestigious brick and stone two-story that stood out along the tree-lined street had captured her admiration as a child and became her dream that one day it would be hers.

O'Malley Investigations occupied the first floor on the west side of the building. A hallway separated her office from the apartment rented out to Mrs. Henricks, a widow Samantha adored. She brought back memories of her own mother: neat, creative, an easy smile and dry wit. In her kitchen, Mrs. Henricks would bake huge cinnamon rolls and brought them to Sam's office every Friday morning.

No one called in sick Friday! The newly renovated studio apartment on the second floor became Samantha's home. Remodeling and leasing out the rest of the floor would eventually provide revenue to pay for upkeep on the building. Samantha gathered the mail from the wall box in the breezeway and climbed the stairway to her apartment.

Unlocking the door, she hung her coat and hat on the coat tree and tossed her keys and gloves into the wicker basket by the table lamp. Arthur, her gray Persian cat, came running around the corner and rubbed against her leg.

"Hey, buddy, bet your food dish is empty. Seems like I haven't been home for days." Arthur hung on the kitchen drawer closure watching her prepare his meal. "This should hold you for a while. Arthur, you eat better than I do…certainly with more regularity!" The soft, gentle, nonbusiness side of Samantha always appeared when she dealt with her loyal pet.

Shedding her slacks and sweater, Samantha headed for the newly tiled bathroom, the latest room that had been remodeled. Water burst from the shower head into the Victorian tub while she pinned her long blond hair into a bun on top of her head. Pulling a fresh towel from the shelf and draping it over a hook, she stepped into the tub and laid back in the hot water.

The sensual herbal bath salts that she had added to the water took Samantha to her favorite tropical fantasy. The fizz from the salts cleared her senses, removed the early spring chill, and silenced the echoes of people describing dead bodies in alleys with no motives or suspects. The fantasy led her to an uninhabited island where gentle waves of water danced on white sand and tickled her toes.

She could see a man in the distance with open arms beckoning her to come to him. Just then the phone rang bringing reality back. She quickly pulled herself up, wrapped the towel around her and stepped out of the tub. She rushed to the phone saying,

"It's got to be Andy. God, don't let him hang up before I get there."

"Hello?"

"Hello, sweetheart, leaving for work?" Andy asked, hoping to surprise her.

"Andy, it's so good to hear your voice. I hope you're at O'Hare."

"No, babe, I'm still in South America. The contractor is pushing to get a concrete pour in before the weather turns. We are already four days behind schedule and a tropical storm is predicted. I can't leave until this is accomplished. The reception is bad here...the storm is coming inland. I need to go, babe. I love you."

The phone went dead before she could respond. Samantha replaced the phone receiver and turned toward her bed. "It's just you and me, Arthur. For the whole weekend...damn it!" Arthur was already curled up on the comforter purring. He didn't seem to mind at all that Andy wasn't going to be there. She set the alarm for an hour nap and curled up under the comforter.

One year earlier, Andrew Courson, owner of Courson Construction, had met Samantha at a job site. A steel worker had fallen to his death and rumors circulated that the worker had been pushed off the edge. Samantha was hired to investigate the death by Andy's insurance company. After three weeks of litigation, the jury came back with a hung verdict. It wasn't a feather in her hat, but she had left an indelible mark on them.

Shortly after the case, she accepted a dinner date with Andy on the condition they didn't talk shop. When Andy removed the hard hat and dressed in stylish clothes, Samantha found him attractive. His charisma, humor, and good looks captured Samantha's heart. Whenever Andy was in the Chicago area, he would call her, and it wasn't long before the two of them fell in love.

He stayed with her when he was checking job sites in Chicago or catching connecting flights for meetings at the New York home office. And he always made time to check on Mrs. Henricks.

The obnoxious alarm caused Samantha to open one eye long enough to reach over and knock the clock off the nightstand in an effort to silence it. It didn't work.

"Okay, okay, I'm awake," Samantha said as she threw the covers back and padded her way to the deck doors that looked out over Oak Street. She glanced out below and saw a woman carrying a Marshall Field shopping bag in the near empty street. Looking the other way, she saw a young couple walking in the street laughing at something funny only to them.

The young woman's arm was around the man's neck and the young man's hand cupped her butt making her jump. It reminded her of when Andy would do that to her, and then he would laugh knowing it embarrassed her. Glancing at her watch, she put away her thoughts of Andy and focused on what she had to do.

2

The sun had almost disappeared over Chicago as Mitch walked up and down both sides of the alley looking for clues that may have been overlooked during the initial search. Shining a flashlight, he looked for possible blood spatter along the graffiti-covered brick walls. Nothing.

Samantha got out of her parked car, pulled the collar of her raincoat tighter around her neck, and hurried across the street. Seeing Samantha walk toward him, Mitch held the crime tape up so she could enter the area. Cops, still at the scene nodded to her. They remembered her from the academy and the force and applauded her courage and determination to strike out on her own.

"I compared the Kramer case to the Himmey Miller murder, and the similarities are numerous, Sam. Different days, places and times are the only variables. Both successful, well-respected businessmen. All the same age, give or take a couple of years," Mitch stated when she was beside him.

"There was a cigarette butt and what looked like a dirty clasp of some kind in the snow. Maybe off a suitcase or briefcase. I'll send both to the lab. Maybe they can get DNA or a fingerprint from them."

Samantha studied the alley from one end to the other. Dead rats by garbage cans, live rats scurrying to safety, broken cheap whiskey bottles, yellow stains in frozen snow from winos the night before, and used heroin syringes made up the open-air coffin Otto Kramer was laid to rest in. Sam found no such indication of shoe tracks and drag marks in the slush that were distinctive enough to suggest the body had been dragged to the alley.

She did find a shoe heel print that was very unusual, close to where the body had been found. The print was preserved and positioned in the frozen slush such that neither the sun nor the building vents had not thawed it. That was it for clues.

"Mitch, did anyone get a picture of this heel mark?"

"Levi didn't say anything about it. I'll take some."

After taking pictures from several angles, Mitch pulled his notebook out and resumed giving Samantha specifics he had been given by the two officers that found Mr. Kramer.

"Mueller estimates Kramer left the store after 0135 because they went by the store on another call at 0122 and lights were on. She thinks he turned left to walk to his car, which he always parked behind the building. He was apparently by himself. Only one set of tracks. Shoe patterns matching the rubber boots he had over his high-top boots were definitely made after the snow fall last night but they end at the alley entrance."

"Stop! You said Kramer had boots on over his shoes, right?" Samantha asked.

"Yeah, that's right…why?"

"Well, why were the boots taken off? And where are they? What was so special about the shoes that the boots were removed?" Samantha's hunger for details and points of interest was kicking in. "And the heel print was that of a shoe heel, so the boots were removed while Kramer was standing up," Samantha thought out loud.

"That makes sense. His shoes were still on when he was found," Mitch added.

Mitch continued with his notes. "The TOD is thought to be around 0140 to 0150 according to the medical examiner. The probe thermometer showed the body to be 32 degrees, so the ME couldn't be positive about time of death. Mueller and Morton responded to the call at 0239. They thought he was totally frozen then."

"Morton had to have had a hell of a mess peeling Kramer off the ground, though the ambulance attendants probably thawed him some before he was removed. There is no evidence of a struggle, no defensive wounds on his hands and nothing under his nails. The lab will be able to confirm that." Mitch closed his notebook and walked over to Samantha.

"Wonder why Otto left so late?" Sam was thinking about the hour the store lights were on and when he was found. "Had any of the patrol units noticed lights on so late after closing? That surely wasn't common for him or the other victim."

"I don't know, Sam, I'll check. It wasn't robbery. A wedding ring, an expensive watch still running, a money clip with money, car keys, all in his coat pocket that was laying off to his side…certainly doesn't suggest robbery. He was either surprised, or worse, knew his killer."

"What about his office? What kind of shape was it in?"

"Sgt. Mueller said it looked normal. Neat, nothing out of place. The safe was unopened. The only tracks were Kramer's as he rounded the corner into the alley; although, if there were others, they may have been intentionally brushed away."

Deep in thought, Samantha finally spoke after several minutes of silence. "These two murders…are personal, Mitch. Very, very personal!"

Samantha and Mitch made a final sweep of the alley and walked to their cars. The streetlights on Michigan now highlighted the dirty snow that remained in the alley. The dinner hour was approaching and people were headed home from work.

"How about spaghetti at the Gillini house?" Mitch could see the serious expression on Samantha's face and wished to change it to the million-dollar smile that usually graced her face.

"You love Mom's pasta and garlic bread. It's Saturday night, and that's always the special. What else have you got to do?"

"Not tonight, Mitch. I have this damn case filling my mind. I'm really drained. I'm thinking a glass of wine and bed sounds better than a meal. Tell your parents hi for me and maybe next week. See ya Monday."

Samantha got in her car and closed the door, dodging any further conversation and headed home. The city was full of shoppers, sight-seekers, and one more unexplained homicide.

Mitch, like Samantha, came from a long line of Chicago police officers. His great-grandfather, fresh from Italy and speaking English with a heavy accent, was present during the Great Chicago Fire of 1871. Every Saturday night, the Gillini family came together for spaghetti at the 4th generation family house.

After the feast, great-grandfather Gillini and his brothers would gather the little ones in a circle by the fireplace and tell cop and robber stories until it was time to leave. Mitch's grandfather and father carried on the tradition through the years. When Mitch's time came, he would retell the tales to nieces and nephews only adding his own version of how his father helped to catch Al Capone.

The Capone stories warranted stern looks from his mother who knew they were so far off the truth. But the kids were entertained.

Mitch had partnered with Samantha shortly after she was off probation with the department.

The match was good both professionally and personally. Their temperaments were much the same and both had spotless records on the force. Samantha had formed a bond with Mitch early. He bore all the investigative qualities that Samantha looked for. They maintained a professional relationship when working together, but on weekends, they would meet for a beer or have a meal at the Gillini family home.

He was the only one, outside of Andy, who got away with calling her Sam. When she left the force and started her own business, she asked Mitch to be a partner in her agency. He declined but agreed to do side work for her. He had too many years on the force to quit. And staying until retirement age would afford him a comfortable retirement.

Walking up the steps to her apartment, only then did she realize how tired she really was. Her boots felt two sizes too small for her feet and a nagging ache had formed in the back of her head. She ignored the blinking light on her phone indicating messages, poured a glass of wine and plopped down in front of the TV to watch the news coverage of the Kramer murder.

3

Monday morning promised to be a pretty spring day. Samantha lowered her car window to smell the fresh air as she drove to the city morgue to meet Mitch. She pressed the entrance button and spoke into the wall microphone.

"Detectives Samantha O'Malley and Mitch Gillini to see Dr. Rudolph Cullen."

An obnoxious buzzer sounded, and the door lock released allowing them entrance to the dull gray corridor that led to the room where bodies would serve as a puzzle with missing pieces. Dr. Cullen would work his genius in putting all the pieces together that would lead to telling how the bodies met their demise.

The city morgue had two coroners and usually an intern working around the clock. Dr. Cullen was Samantha's favorite and whose findings she always accepted in questionable deaths. He had known her father well and even attended BBQs that her parents had hosted for the neighborhood. She had seen enough autopsy procedures to be immune to the distasteful procedure.

Mitch, on the other hand, had avoided autopsies knowing his stomach couldn't handle watching one performed.

"Good morning, Detectives," Sally Preston, the coroner's secretary, greeted both detectives with a warm smile and sparkling eyes. "Dr. Cullen has already entered the autopsy lab. He just signed on the recording microphone. Your timing is perfect." Sally handed them visitor passes and buzzed the observation room door open.

"What's good about it? I hate these things," Mitch said under his breath. "A good morning to me is being in Florida fishing!"

"Think clinical, Mitch. Like it was never a person," Samantha suggested as they walked to the observation deck.

Samantha took a seat in front of the viewing window and watched Dr. Cullen mesh his gloved fingers together to ensure they were all the way on and surveyed the rest of the room. On the steel table was the covered body of Otto Kramer. It had already been weighed. An identification number logged and tagged the race, sex, approximate age, and name of the victim recorded by the intern when the body was brought to the morgue.

A bright light shining against the wall highlighted the various tools that hung in clear plastic sheaths. On a wheeled cart graduated sizes of operating knives laid in order of use by the medical examiner. A test tube rack would be used to hold tissue, blood, and bone samples. A black hose was secured to a swing mount that would wash away excess body fluids.

A smaller table placed to the right of Dr. Cullen would hold organs that might be sectioned. Steel scales hung above the dissecting table to weigh organs. A microphone hung from the ceiling recording Dr. Cullen's notes for the secretary's copy. That copy would be used in court if necessary.

Sinks at the foot of the metal table provided a place to wash gloved hands and tools. A block had been placed under Otto Kramer's head so blood would drain away from the head region.

Dr. Cullen introduced himself into the hanging microphone and gave the date and time of the autopsy. He introduced the intern that would assist him and the name and condition of the victim's body. He glanced at the observation room and saw Samantha. He asked the intern to turn down the sound.

"Detective O'Malley, it is good to see you again. I believe that is Detective Gillini with you today, correct? This is a nasty case, I'm afraid, but Cook County has the best detectives on the case. Together we will give his story an ending, though it won't be a pleasant one."

Samantha waved and smiled back at Dr. Cullen and listened intently as the autopsy began. He motioned for the sound to be turned up.

"Case number H-9. The 'H' indicates a homicide case. The '9' means the ninth homicide in Cook County this year. The skin from the chest, back, and thighs have been removed meticulously as if done by a medical professional. Surface blood samples have been taken for bacteriological and chemical analyses. The report is not back at this time."

"Oral and nasal swabs have been taken, as well as fingernail scrapings and are currently in the lab. The tissue and pores of the nasal cavity were shrunk indicating some type of chemical had been introduced to the region. I will begin the 'Y' incision," Dr. Cullen stated.

Taking a scalpel, Dr. Cullen made the incision from the shoulder to mid-chest and down to the pubic region. He examined the heart and lungs and found them to appear normal. Taking a large needle and syringe, he drew blood from both organs and handed the syringe to his intern to be capped and sent to the lab.

Using the Virchow method, he removed the intestines and cut primary organs that were removed using the method and a small section to be placed in a container and sent to the lab. He followed the same procedure with the lungs, liver, and thyroid gland, then addressed the audience.

"I am having these samples sent to the lab to be checked for poisons that may have been given to the victim. The organs will be documented as appearing healthy and determined not part of the cause of death at this time," Dr. Cullen explained.

A rubber block was placed under the shoulder to hyper-flex the neck allowing the spine to arch backward and the chest moved forward. This gave Dr. Cullen the best exposure to the trunk of the body. Moving to the end of the table, Dr. Cullen removed the body block to begin the brain autopsy. He made a cut from the bony section behind the right ear, across the crown of the head, down to the small bump behind the left ear.

The cranium was opened with a saw exposing the soft tissue. After removing the brain and examining the tissue, Dr. Cullen noted nothing abnormal. With expertise, he encapsulated the tissue back into the skull and sealed it.

The intern took the organs that were removed and bagged them. Setting them aside, he lined the body cavity with a cotton material and placed the bagged organs inside.

Taking the overhead shower from the mount, he washed the entire body. Dr. Cullen made a final pass over the body and nodded for the intern to take the signed hard copy of the autopsy report to the secretary.

When the autopsy was totally complete, Dr. Cullen's intern sewed the body back up. Turning off the recorder, Dr. Cullen removed his gloves, stepped around the autopsy table, and looked up at Samantha and Mitch. "With what I know now, it is my opinion that this man was given a chemical, rendering him unconscious. The skin, as described before, was then removed."

"He froze to death before gaining consciousness. The lab results will be back by Wednesday if not before, and you will be notified of the results by my office. How are you doing, Samantha?" Dr. Cullen asked.

"I'm fine, Doctor, but I'm not sure about Detective Gillini."

"Yes, he does have a greenish tint to his skin color, doesn't he?" Dr. Cullen chuckled and walked toward the exit door. The intern placed the body of Otto Kramer back in the cooler.

"How about lunch, Samantha? On me of course," Dr. Cullen asked.

"Thank you. It's been a long time since we've had those neighborhood BBQs that my parents hosted. I have a lot of work to do on these cases and need all the time I can get. I'm requesting a rain check for now. But I do appreciate the offer."

"Request granted. There will be other times. You have a delightful day. Oh, Samantha, my office will contact you personally with the lab results."

Samantha nodded and left the building in search of Mitch. She found him leaning against his car.

"Thank God, that's over. I had to get out of there before I puked!"

"Sorry, Mitch, autopsies take a while to get used to, but I would think with all your years of viewing autopsies on suspicious deaths, you'd be immune to the gore."

"I just can't handle the sawing to open the cranium…reminds me of a dentist drill…that turns my stomach too."

"Some tough guy you are. Come on, wimp. I want to talk with Mrs. Kramer. I'm sure the police have already but I wanted to see the autopsy first."

"Yeah, let's go…I'm fine," Mitch said, gaining his color back. Together, they took Samantha's car and headed for the Chicago suburb the Kramer's lived in.

4

Samantha rang the doorbell to the Kramer's modest suburban home as Mitch surveyed the street. The door opened slowly. "Yes?" A weak voice said. A tall, thin woman stood at the door with no expression on her pale face.

"Mrs. Kramer?"

"Yes."

"Mrs. Kramer, I am Detective O'Malley, and this is Detective Gillini. We are sorry for your loss but need to ask you a few questions about your husband."

"I've already talked to the police," she said with a crisp German accent. "I don't know what I can tell you that is different."

"Yes, we know that, but we want to know more about him and why this happened."

"Alright. Come in," Mrs. Kramer said with hesitation in her voice. She closed the door behind them and led the two to a beautifully furnished room. She took a seat across from them and sat quietly.

"Mrs. Kramer, this is the second death in as many months that has happened to well-known businessmen. Both deaths have had similar characteristics. Detective

Gillini and I are trying to find out why your husband was singled out."

"Like I told the police that were here, I don't know. He was a good man."

"Did Mr. Kramer have any customers that were not happy with him or that would want to harm…"

"NO! Everyone likes Otto! He had a good business and liked everyone! The customers liked him."

"Mrs. Kramer, I know this is a difficult time for you and we apologize for having to interfere with you and your family, but it's important to know why this happened, as well as who did this," Samantha said, trying to calm her down.

"We have no family, Detective. It is or was just Otto and me. We live a simple life and run a good business. That's all."

"I understand, but someone wanted your husband dead. And we need your help to find out who and why."

"Mrs. Kramer, did you and Otto have any issues with any of your neighbors?" Mitch asked.

"We mind our own business and don't bother anyone," Mrs. Kramer said, getting annoyed at the questioning.

"Was it common for Mr. Kramer to work so late?"

"Sometimes. It is inventory time, and a sale will come shortly after, before the spring and summer styles arrive. It is or was a busy time for Otto."

"We believe Mr. Kramer left the store around 1:30 in the morning. Did you know he was going to be working that late?" Samantha asked.

"I go to bed early…I do not always know when Otto comes home," Mrs. Kramer answered, getting agitated at the questions.

Mitch continued to inquire about Otto's work habits and other details while Samantha surveyed the living area of the house. Thick, expensive carpet covered the floor in the living room. The couch they sat on, and the chairs, were upholstered in luxurious fabrics. Antique rugs accented the hardwood floor in the dining room. Books were neatly stacked on the large, marble-topped coffee table.

Draperies made of brightly printed textiles framed the windows. A stone fireplace exposed a large cavity for firewood to be placed but appeared to not have been used in some time. Plants and crystals added life and sparkle to the fireplace mantel. She noticed pink Wedgwood dishes in the ornate corner cabinet and more crystal side dishes on the table.

"I have plans to make," Mrs. Kramer stated sternly. "I need to bury Otto, and I am tired. I think you should go now."

"Maybe another time, Mrs. Kramer," Mitch said as he and Samantha stood up.

"Maybe…we will see," was all Mrs. Kramer said.

Samantha and Mitch gave their thanks for her time and said goodbye as they returned to the car. Both stood outside the car.

"You have that look I've seen before. The one where the wheels are turning in that pretty head of yours. What's that you are thinking?" Mitch asked with an 'I know' grin.

"Did you notice the furnishings in their home? The furniture and upholstery? The China cabinet was filled with expensive Wedgwood dishes. And, oh my God, the carpeting and rugs! And the crystal. None of that says simple life! And I'll bet all her clothes come from Neiman Marcus. And she was always on the defense."

"She sat straight up in the chair, feet flat on the floor. She never looked completely comfortable…more like she was careful not to say more than she had to. Like I said, these murders are personal!"

"What I saw was money and lots of it. Give me your keys. I'll drive," Mitch responded as he pulled away from the curb.

Making a turn down the alley, Mitch explained, "I want to see the backyard…maybe there's a car in the garage."

The backyard was landscaped with shrubs and flower beds still unprepped for spring plantings.

Two trees towered the garage and house. A back door led to a tiered deck that held large flowerpots with remainders of fall bouquets. Not as simple as the front of the house but not outlandish. The garage door was down and shades to the garage windows were still lowered.

"Where to now, lady? You're thinking about something, and I know better than to ask."

Samantha remained silent and stared out the car door window.

"If you don't need me," Mitch said, breaking the silence, "I'll go back to the morgue and get my car. I'm going home and get some sleep. It's been a long night for me, and you aren't going to talk."

"Yeah, that's fine, Mitch. I'll talk to you later. Hey, tomorrow, see if you can pull any duty reports and evidence logs on Officers Mueller and Morton for the nights of the two murders. I want to see if one or the other took time off before or after the Miller and Kramer murders."

"What are you thinking?" Mitch asked before closing the car door, but he could tell Sam had no intention of sharing what was on her mind. "You know, you piss me off sometimes. I'm supposed to be your partner, yet you won't talk to me like one! Hell, you just don't say anything! What are you thinking?"

"I'm not talking…remember?" Samantha answered with a wink as he left the car.

5

The clanging office door chimes announced Samantha's entrance. "Hey! Good morning, Samantha!" Heather said as she looked up from her work. "Two calls for you already…here are the notes on them," she said, handing them over to her. Heather and Samantha had met in college before Samantha left for the police academy.

Their friendship developed over the years, and Heather had excelled in her career working for oil company executives but was ready for a change. When Samantha told Heather she was opening her own business, Heather applied for the position of receptionist and secretary.

Samantha skimmed through the notes and decided they could wait before a response was needed. She checked her mailbox in the hall and climbed the stairs to her apartment. Tossing her keys in the basket, she kicked off her shoes and laid her purse on the couch. Arthur came running from his bed meowing at her as if disgruntled.

"Is complain all you can do, mister? How about 'how was your day' or 'glad to see you home'?" Smiling, she went to her desk.

Thinking about the Himmey Miller case, she called the record department.

"Jami, how ya' doing? O'Malley here. You still owe me a beer. Thursday night? Jami, you always pick the 2 for 1 nights. Yeah, yeah, yeah…you got a family, your mother-in-law is in the hospital, and your dog has diarrhea…can't you come up with something new?" Laughter followed.

"Jami, would you print off a copy of the evidence sheet on the Himmey Miller murder two months back? I want to compare it to the Otto Kramer murder a few nights ago. Good. Mitch will pick it up later today. Thanks."

She placed the receiver back and pulled Arthur down on her lap. "Why does life have to be so hard, Arthur? Why can't it be live, laugh and love?"

Finishing a quick lunch, she picked up the top note Heather had given her, studied it, and called the number.

"Afternoon. Detective O'Malley returning a call from the chief."

"One moment, Detective. I'll see if he is available," Katrina, the chief's secretary said.

"Hello, Miss O'Malley. I will make this brief. I would like to use your agency in solving the Kramer murder. I understand there are significant similarities to the Miller case you are involved in."

"I'll take the Kramer case along with the Miller case, Chief, as long as it is understood that I am leading the investigation and that I have the full cooperation from your officers and that my people have full access to any records, files, and evidence pertaining to both cases."

With a long pause on his end, the chief agreed to the conditions.

"Keep me in the loop, O'Malley…" But the chief didn't get a chance to finish his sentence.

Samantha smiled as she replaced the receiver. "I'll bet he's clenching his fists and cussing!"

Samantha walked to the balcony and opened both French doors. Leaning over the balcony, she watched people walking on the sidewalk. She listened to the giggles and chatter of children playing hopscotch in the adjacent parking lot. A truck with an open flatbed hauling large cylinder-shaped tanks of water drove slowly down Oak Street and disappeared onto Lake Shore Drive.

The sight of them reminded her of the library pictures of the cylinders of CO gas that were piped into the chambers filled with Jews awaiting their deaths. The Holocaust had been the subject for her college thesis. She turned back to the children playing and thought how lucky they were to be in America with no such worries to deal with. She walked back in and closed the doors.

Troubling thoughts lingered in her mind. She glanced at her watch and saw she had time to drive to the library and view more footage of the death camps.

6

Across town in a small building on a side street, a nervous man walks into a wood-paneled office. A window overlooking the street gave light to the somber room. Plants trailing down from tall bookcases were the only signs of life beyond the presence of the two men.

"Well, it's good to see you again. You missed your appointment last week."

"Yes, I know. I had things to do."

"What kind of things?"

"Just things that make me happy and had to be taken care of."

"Are you happy now?"

"I think so."

"Are you taking your medication?"

"Most of the time. Sometimes I get irritated and have to take care of things. Then I don't."

"But that is when you should take it. It will keep you calmer, and you won't feel like you have to take care of things, as you say."

"Stop it! You don't know what it is like…to be the one to take care of these things. Nobody else is doing it."

"Can you get someone to help you?"

"No, I'm the only one. They wouldn't understand either." He rubbed his sweaty hands on his jeans.

"We can talk about something else if you want to."

"Yes, I want to talk about the village I lived in. There were nice people there. I played with the neighbor kids. There was a pasture close to the edge of town and we played ball every day after school. We were popular, as we spoke some German and some English. My father only spoke Yiddish."

"My mother wanted me to adopt more modern ways and to dress in more modern styles, but I dressed mostly in traditional clothes to please my father. I had many friends in our town. Then they came and made us quit."

"Who came?"

"The soldiers."

"Why?"

"They told us we were moving."

"Did they tell you why?"

"No, but my parents knew. They were told."

"You told me your father had a men's clothing shop. Did he have to close the store before the move?"

"He was one of many who had to close their businesses. The Metzer's owned a China store and a jewelry store. They were very good friends of my parents. Their stores closed. My family's best friend, Mr. Kirshner, owned a men's store. He did on-site tailoring for his customers. It made everyone sad when he had to close his store. The soldiers made all the businesses close."

"At our last meeting, you said your mother allowed you to take a toy with you. Is that right?"

"Yes. Just one. I wanted to take my puppy, so I carried him inside my coat when we left the house."

"Did your parents know you had the puppy and not a toy?"

"No. My father was already out in the street, and my mother was crying and holding her stomach when she took me out of the house. I thought she was sick. She didn't see me hide the puppy."

"So you and your mother joined your father on the street?"

"Yes. It was cold outside. So very cold. The soldier said everyone had to leave until the war was over, and then we would be coming home."

"So, this was during the war?"

"YES! I told you that at our first meeting. Are you trying to confuse me?" The man said tapping his shoes on the floor and running his hand through his hair as if agitated.

"No, no. I want to be sure I understand you. Now, where did you go when you left your home?"

"I don't know where we went. It was getting dark, and I followed the others with my parents. We walked to the edge of town to the train tracks and were told to get in the long train cars. A soldier came up to me and wanted to know what I had inside my coat. I told him a loaf of bread. He slapped my face hard, knocking me backward."

"The puppy's tail was hanging out from under my coat and he saw it. He made me take him out and put him on the ground. He was lost in the crowd of people boarding the train cars. I don't know what happened to him. I just know I never saw him again."

"Tell me about the train cars."

"They were dirty and smelly. Too many people were crowded in them. My mother was pulled away from me. She had to get into a line with other women and girls that got into a different train car. I just saw the back of her coat. I needed to use the bathroom but there weren't any. I peed on my shoes…they were new."

"Were you the only little boy in the train car?"

"There were other kids. Most were my age and younger. One teenage boy I didn't know. I could hear some of them crying…the very young ones."

"Were you afraid?"

"I wasn't worried then. I thought maybe it was some kind of a vacation, but not like the other ones we took when we went to the mountains to ski."

"How long were you on the train?"

"A long time. It was totally dark and my legs were cramping. There was no place to sit down and my feet were cold."

"What happened when the train stopped?"

"I have already told you that too! You must listen to me! I was helped off the train because I couldn't walk right. My legs were cramping and my feet were so cold. A soldier with a big dog was shouting orders. I didn't understand everything he said, so I just followed the others and looked for my parents in the crowd of people. I couldn't see them anywhere."

"Where did you go when you got off the train?"

"We were divided up. All boys were led to a long building with windows and a small light at the entrance of it. We were in building 8. The Jewish boys in that building were high risk. If we had brown hair and brown eyes, we had a tattoo on our arm. If the boys had blond hair and blue eyes, they did not get a tattoo. I learned later that no tattoo meant they lived. I believe the same was true for the girls."

"The girls went with their mothers. I don't know where they went. I was getting scared. I was tired and hungry and had soiled my pants. I didn't have any more clothes with me. I wanted my mother, she would know what to do."

"You are getting upset. Do you want to stop here and talk more the next time?"

"Yes. I don't want to remember anymore now." Beads of sweat had formed on his forehead.

"Here is a handkerchief...wipe your forehead. It's alright to cry if you want to."

"I've already done that. I need to go. Goodbye."

7

The sun was leaning to the west when Samantha left the library and headed home. She knew looking through the footage at the library could be like finding a needle in a haystack, but she had to follow her instincts. Samantha had taken detailed notes on Nazi atrocities and was anxious to compare the notes to the two murder cases she was working on. The air was warm enough for her to lower her car window.

As she approached Clark Street, several emergency vehicles blocked traffic from passing. Detour signs were posted on both sides of the street. A fire hose stretched across the street to a warehouse. All the people working at the scene were dressed in contaminated protective clothing. She slowed and waited for her turn to take the detour. At the intersection, a patrol officer motioned for her to drive forward. As she approached the officer, he greeted her.

"Hi, Miss O'Malley."

She thought she recognized him. It was Levi Kanter. "What happened, Levi?"

"Chemical spill is all I know."

"Chemicals in that warehouse? It was condemned years ago!" Samantha stated.

“That’s all I know about it.” Levi blew his whistle to get the traffic moving and Samantha drove on.

All the way to her office, Samantha was deep in thought. She wondered why chemicals were being stored in a condemned building that the city had done nothing about tearing down.

What was the chemical and how did it spill? She would store the questions in her mind and add them to her library notes when she got home. The building hadn’t been used in ten or more years and the property had been ignored by the city way too long. Traffic was slow in the congested area. When it came to a stop, Samantha glanced around at the cars parked along the curbs.

One of the cars had a passenger sitting in the front seat…no one else in the vehicle. As she inched forward, she glanced at the car and passenger. It looked like Levi’s car and from the side mirror, she saw the face of Sgt. Mueller sitting in it.

Why were night shift officers working the spill? There were enough evening shift personnel to cover it. Why those two from nights? Just more questions she had to find answers to.

Mrs. Henrick was raking leaves away from her flower beds when Samantha got out of her car.

“Good evening, Samantha! Been keeping long hours at work?”

“Unfortunately, it goes with the territory, Mrs. Henrick. A little early to be clearing off the flower beds, isn’t it? April can be fickle, you know.”

“I’m tired of winter and it is so nice out now. The jonquils and tulips are peeking through the ground, so I want to give them a little air and sunlight," Mrs. Henrick said with a smile.

Agatha's flowers brought color to the landscape around the building in the spring and summer, and Samantha loved how they softened the front side of the building. She glanced in the window to her office and saw that Heather had already left, the lights were off and the door locked. Just ads in her mailbox. Maybe a quiet night was in store for her.

She could hear her phone ringing as she hurriedly climbed the steps to her apartment. Once inside, she grabbed the phone with the hope that the caller was a special someone.

"Hello?" Samantha said.

"Hey, lover…let's get naked and make mad, passionate love!"

"Andy, don't tease me! You're a continent away from me and probably another huge delay in returning to Chicago! I would like nothing more than to be in your arms and…"

"Good, because I'm at O'Hare right now," Andy said, shutting her off.

"I'll come get you right now."

"No, I'm renting a car and will be there in an hour at the most. Be appropriately undressed for me and have your door unlocked." Andy smiled as he hung up before she could say anything.

Once the door slowly closed, a look of wanton passion held their eyes. Instead of words Andy pulled Samantha into a soft embrace and kissed her tenderly. He let her go and looked into her eyes. The message was clear. He pulled her to him again. Their lips, open and hot, met in a long passionate kiss not to be broken. He held her naked body tighter running his hand down the curve of her waist and back.

Feeling his arousal, she lifted a long, smooth leg around him exposing her need for him. His hand moved to cup her hip and then gently further down to the warm, wet treasure he wanted to have. He cradled her in his arms. He could feel her heart beating and kissed her forehead as he lifted her up in his arms and carried her to the bedroom and gently laid her on the bed. She watched him undress and join her as the hunger grew.

Andy pulled her to him and kissed her face, her neck and shoulder. Samantha's breathing became more pronounced as she draped one long leg over him. Andy moved down to kiss the soft skin between her breasts then cupped one in his hand and circled the hard nipple with his tongue. She moaned as she dug her fingers in the small of his back.

He continued to lick her skin knowing her arousal was growing. She took both hands and tried to push him between her opened legs.

"Not yet," he whispered. "I'm not done." He moved to her navel and kissed the trembling flesh around it. His hand slowly eased down her thigh and back up to her hip. Gently, he turned on his back and pulled her on top of him. She could feel his steady heartbeat unlike the pounding of hers, aching in desire. She could feel his firm muscles under her and his hardness.

She kissed him hard lacing her fingers in his hair and tried to shift her body down to it, but Andy held her tight, not letting her move down.

"I said I wasn't done," he said softly and rolled her over on her back once again. "I want to taste all of you." Andy held her waist as he worked his way to the soft, moist area. Samantha trembled with passion and cried out.

"Andy, please…I want you…all of you! Now!"

Andy entered her with a tender rhythm that grew faster, sending Samantha into a burst of passion. She cried out and begged for more. Andy, wanting to please her, brought her to a peak again and together they shared their release. Holding each other afterward, they drifted off to sleep still wrapped in each other's arms.

Samantha opened the French doors that led to the balcony and smelled the dewy morning perfume from the cherry blossoms across the street. She looked beautiful in a sheer white night gown. The sun followed her curves as the light breeze blew the gown's folds and lifted the soft curls of her blond hair. May Day was going to be as beautiful as she was.

Andy appeared through the doors carrying a tray holding two mugs of coffee and scones. He set the tray on the wicker table, walked over to her, and kissed her neck.

"What a gorgeous morning. Just like my lady."

"Mmmmm. You are going to make a wonderful husband," Samantha murmured.

"Are you proposing?" Andy asked looking at her.

"Nope. And you know why. Although after last night, it's becoming harder to decline."

"Absence makes the heart grow fonder you know. But I can wait…the prize is well worth it," Andy said with a grin. "So, what's on the docket for today?"

"Andy, something very strange is going on with these two homicides. I was at the library earlier this week doing research on some WWII facts, and I'm smelling a connection between the two murders and something the Nazis did to some of the Jews during the Holocaust. Then, coming home, traffic was stalled on Clark Street. There had been a chemical spill in an abandoned building."

"I saw Levi's car with Sgt. Mueller sitting in it parked on the side street that was part of the traffic detour. I don't understand why he and Mueller were there. They work nights. There were plenty of evening shift police to handle the situation. Something isn't right but I can't put my finger on it yet."

"I'm waiting on the results of some lab tests on the physical evidence today…but I've got to get inside that building."

"Is there anything I can do to help? I just have a meeting this morning but I'm free this afternoon," Andy offered.

"No, I just don't know enough yet. Let's have dinner tonight. Maybe I'll know more then." The Michigan Lake breeze became stronger, so Samantha put on the matching robe to her nightgown. The irksome rattling of a car engine broke the thoughts in Samantha's head as the car pulled up along the curb by the apartment building.

"Hey up there. Are you two decent? I could sure use some coffee if there is any left."

Mitch saw the two on the balcony from the sidewalk. As usual, he was there to pick up Samantha.

"If you hurry!" Andy answered.

"Andy, good to see you, man. And good morning, boss!" Mitch said as he walked onto the balcony. "Andy, did you watch the Cubs and Cincinnati ballgame last night?"

"Ah no, I was pretty occupied," Andy said with a sheepish smile.

Finishing her coffee and taking the tray toward the balcony door, she looked back at the two men. "I'll leave you two misfits to discuss baseball while I dress for work." Samantha laughed and returned inside.

"The sanitation department this morning, right, Sam?" Mitch hollered to her.

"Yep…first thing followed by checking out a condemned building. Hope you aren't tired, it's going to be a long morning."

8

Mitch parked his car in the city's sanitation department parking lot, and he and Samantha walked to the office.

"Good morning. Detective O'Malley and Gillini to see Frank Simpson," Samantha said to the receptionist.

Checking her logbook, the receptionist responded. "Frank is not back yet from his route. Oh, is this about the body he found?"

"Yes," answered Samantha.

"I can radio him to come in if it's that important, but he'll be in for the day in about twenty minutes," the receptionist offered.

"We can wait."

Minutes later, the two detectives saw several sanitation trucks pull into the yard. As Mitch and Samantha walked in that direction, a tall man approached them.

"I'm Frank Simpson. I was told you were looking for me."

"Mr. Simpson…"

"Frank please."

"Detectives O'Malley and Gillini," Samantha said showing her credentials. "We want to ask you some questions about the body you saw. Frank, tell us why you were in the alley and what you saw by Kramer's Men's Store."

"I'll tell you what I know," Frank Simpson stated. "It wasn't a routine stop on my route. Buddy Wilson is supposed to stop there but called in sick…flu or something. Our dispatcher asked if I was close enough to pick the trash up at Kramer's. It wasn't a problem for me. When I got there…"

"What time was that?" Samantha asked.

"Well, it was around 2:20 to 2:25 a.m., I think. Should be on my log and the dispatcher's log. I can go check."

"We will do that. Then what?"

"I backed my truck into the alley like I would at any of my stops. I walked over to check the dumpster and saw what looked like someone lying about midway in the alley. It's nothing to find a bum camped out in the alleys, but the noise of the truck usually wakes them and they move to the side of the alley. That dude didn't move! I walked down to see why."

"I guess seeing him stretched out like that looked odd. I always carry a flashlight with me…rats, you know. I held the light on him and saw just raw flesh…no skin. And he looked frozen. I felt sick. Got back in my truck, and radioed in where I was and what I found. I waited for the police and as soon as they were done questioning me, I got the hell out of there. Never want to see anything like that again!"

"You told the police the same thing?" Mitch asked.

"Yep. Check it out."

"We will, Frank, and thanks for your time. We appreciate it," Mitch said.

"No problem. I haven't clocked out yet. A little OT, you know." Frank grinned as he waved to them.

"What do you think, Mitch?" Samantha asked when Frank was out of sight.

"I think he's straight, but I'll get a copy of the police report and the dispatcher's to get the time of the call and his written version."

"Mitch, go back to the department and see if the tab has made a match on the heel print you took a picture of. Cindy, the lab tech, called but the connection was so bad, I didn't get all that she said. Then meet me at that old, condemned warehouse on Clark Street."

"10-4. Oh, you still want the logs on Officer Morton and Sgt. Mueller's shifts?"

"Absolutely."

Mitch took Samantha back to her office. Once inside her apartment, she changed into old jeans and a hooded sweatshirt. She put boots on over her loafers thinking the building could be wet on the inside. She checked her .45 and put it in the waistband holster.

When she got to the condemned building, she parked in the back and looked for an unlocked door. Finding one at the far end of the dock, she walked in. It was dark and damp. Everything was quiet. Using her flashlight, she looked at the walls and large pillars that supported the building. Several windows had been broken out and a few sparrows were flying overhead.

Condensation drops fell from overhead piping and melodiously pooled into several puddles through the building floor.

Reaching the far end of the room, the light beam of her flashlight caught what looked like a metal door handle to an oversized door. Samantha walked toward the door, stopped, and listened for any noise. Nothing. At eye-level, she could see a small hole drilled into the steel door. No one there. She turned the doorknob and pulled the door open just enough for her to see inside.

Her eyes became accustomed to the semi-darkness and traveled around the visible area. Smaller, partitioned areas were all that she could see. Curious to know the purpose, she opened the door wide enough to get through it. She closed the door quietly behind her, still not satisfied that the building was empty.

She walked to the smaller rooms and examined them. Each was made of two-inch thicknesses of plywood. All the doors to each room were equipped with a locking mechanism. All but one of the doors were locked with new-looking locks. She opened the door to the unlocked one.

There were two primitively built benches in the middle of the room, one solitary light bulb overhead, an overhead pipe running the width of the room with spigots every two feet, and a drain in the middle of the floor. A hole had been drilled in the two upper side walls for the piping to continue to the next room. Samantha studied the drain, spigots, and piping. She knew they were not part of the original building.

"Oh my God! Oh my God!" She whispered to herself.

Samantha's heart pounded and sweat formed on her forehead. Cold chills ran the course of her entire body. She covered her mouth with her hand to prevent the gasp that had formed deep in her throat. Fear gripped her entire body.

Leaving everything the way she found it, she hurried to the door she entered and opened it just enough to be sure no one else was in the parking area. Getting back in her car, she drove to the corner and put the car in the park until her legs quit shaking and she had control again. In that cold, lifeless building, she knew her instincts had led her well. She drove to Mitch's apartment and ran up the stairs.

"Mitch, I know what is going on! Get your stuff and come with me. I need to use your phone before we leave." She called Andy's office and talked with his secretary.

"Hi, Jean. Is Andy there? Oh, well, please tell him dinner is on hold, and I will get back with him. Thanks." She hung up.

"Well, can I at least throw a shirt on? I was sleeping, you know," Mitch asked sarcastically.

"Yeah, just hurry."

Coming out of his bedroom, he grabbed his coat and held the apartment door open as Samantha hurried through. Together, they returned to the warehouse. Once inside, she led the way to the side room she found earlier. Opening the door cautiously, she spoke softly to Mitch.

"Look in here and tell me what you think it is."

Mitch took his flashlight out and shined it on the walls, ceiling, benches, and piping hanging from the ceiling.

"I don't believe it. It's a model gas chamber! Everything is here except the crematorium and people to put in it," Mitch said in a low voice.

"I came here earlier this afternoon to figure out why there was a chemical spill in here and who is storing chemicals. This is what I found!"

"Let's keep looking around. This is a big place," Mitch said.

"There is a set of stairs I saw earlier, but when I found this room, I didn't go up. Go quietly in case we aren't alone in here."

Together, they climbed to the second floor. There were light switches and a breaker box by the door. Mitch surveyed the room and saw a shadow under the door. With his hand, he unsnapped his gun holster and placed his hand on the butt. Pulling the door open, expecting a person, he cautiously stepped inside, but there was nothing but a pair of black rubber boots on the floor,

Mitch and Samantha moved along the wall and could see large cylinders lined up against it.

Mitch looked for labels to identify them. They were clean of all writing but piping led from the regulators on the cylinders to a narrow pipe running along the wall. From there, it went down and through a whole drilled in the cement floor. "Go downstairs to the unlocked room and see where the pipe went," Mitch said.

"The pipe is connected to the piping that has the spigots attached overhead, Mitch," she said when she joined him upstairs.

"This is big, Mitch. Who would want to copy such a thing? We need to know what's in the cylinders along the wall. Let's go back and look closer at them."

"There isn't anything identifying the contents," Mitch said when they returned to where the cylinders were stored. "Maybe they were left by the former owners of this warehouse. I don't dare open the regulator without knowing what is in these. Let's go. I'll try and find out who the previous owners were." Mitch looked the cylinders over one more time and checked the back of them.

"Whoa! Here's a partial tag. It looks like it's been laying in water but there's something legible on it." Picking the tag up off the floor, he shone his flashlight on it. "I can see a 'C' but can't read the rest of it. I think there might be a 'Y' and an 'N' but can't be sure. It's real faded," Mitch said.

"Hydrogen cyanide was used to exterminate the Jews at Auschwitz, Mitch. Maybe that is what is in these cylinders!" Samantha exclaimed. "Are you sure there aren't more tags back there?"

"Yeah. That's it. Just some puddles of water behind here."

"Ok. Let's get out of here…it's almost 10:00. Someone may come," Samantha said as she headed for the dock door. "Can you get someone you trust to spend the night watching if anyone comes here late at night? If you can, I would need pictures of times, car identification, and plates. Have your guy get pictures of their faces too."

9

"I don't want anyone on our force. Right now, I wouldn't trust anyone on our force until we know who is doing this. I know someone in Joliet that would be perfect. I'll call him when we get back," Mitch concluded.

"Joliet? That's a cesspool all its own when it comes to crime. Why Joliet and not one of the suburb departments?"

"Steve Jordon is a detective on the Joliet force. I've known him for years, how he works, and most of all I know he will keep his mouth shut about what's going on," Mitch explained.

"Who would do something like this?" Samantha stated when they were in the car. "It is almost model perfect to what was in Auschwitz. This guy you know…how many nights could he watch the place?"

"Jordon works evenings. He could come here when he's off. It would be dark and there is only one streetlight along that section of the street. He's got a beat-up car that he uses on cases so no one would think too much about it if it was spotted…this area isn't exactly Park Avenue," Mitch said as they pulled out of the parking area and onto the main street.

Samantha dropped Mitch off and drove back to her apartment feeling like she was getting somewhere with the case. She just needed the who and why someone would be skinning the victims.

Early afternoon, Samantha sat in her office comparing Frank Simpson's written police report with the dispatcher's. Both matched. Satisfied with the findings, she moved on to the lab technician's results on the heel print. Just then, the phone rang.

"Samantha, Dr. Cullen calling. Did you read my findings of the shoe heel?"

"Cindy called with the report but the connection was poor, and I didn't get everything she said. I didn't want to bother you, so I sent Mitch after a copy. I'm holding it in my hand right now," Samantha responded.

"Fine. I want you to know it's a perfect match with the picture Mitch gave me! I was very surprised. I also sent the shoes back to the police department to be included with the rest of the evidence," Dr. Cullen said.

"Thank you, Dr. Cullen. That's one thing off my list. Have a good day."

"You too, Samantha." Both hung up.

Arthur stood by the balcony door and meowed.

"You want out, Arthur?" She walked over and opened one of the balcony's French doors.

Arthur moseyed out, jumped up on the balcony wicker chair, and laid down seeming satisfied.

As she closed the door, she noticed a vehicle parked on the opposite side of the street that she thought looked like Officer Levi Kanter's. A man was sitting behind the wheel looking in her direction. He was wearing sunglasses, which he didn't need, and smoking a cigarette. She figured it was coincidental and shook off the notion that it was connected to her.

Returning to her desk, she resumed looking at the lab results. The reports on the shoe heel, which were not in detail, left questions in her mind. She checked the time. She had plenty of time to call Cindy at the lab before she left for the day.

"Chicago Crime Lab, Cindy speaking."

"Cindy, Samantha calling. I am looking at the lab results that you sent with Mitch. Are you positive about the cigarette butt?"

"Yes, and I did further research. The butt was from a Juno brand cigarette that was very popular during WWII and smoked by Nazi officers. I found out they can be purchased in Berlin to this day. There was a trace of DNA in the filter. I have a call into Dr. Cullen to see if he has DNA from Otto Kramer that I can match."

"Good! Let me know ASAP when he responds. Now, what about the heel design?"

"Yep, I got plenty on that! The heel was a common part of shoes worn by high-ranking Nazi officers. The heel design is unique to the shoes they wore. There is a small piece cut out in the middle of the heel that was known to hide a cyanide pill that would be taken if they were captured."

"The design of the heel is unique to only that shoe brand and was made in Munich. Dr. Cullen was to look at the shoes Kramer was wearing to make a match with that."

"Okay. And the fingerprint on the clasp?"

"Nada…smeared and couldn't be checked. Sorry, Samantha."

"Good work, Cindy! Thanks so much. Remember to call me when you know what Dr. Cullen says about the DNA."

"Will do. Bye."

Samantha hung the receiver up, her thoughts swirling in her head. She was beginning to connect the dots. Looking at the stack of mail, she removed the ads, the low interest loan offers, and a letter from her down-state aunt. She would read the letter later. Pulling the comic section out from the newspaper, an index card fell out onto the floor.

Samantha bent down to pick it up and saw a one-line message written in bold black ink on it. 'LEAVE IT ALONE' was all it said. She got an evidence bag from her desk drawer, took the letter opener and without touching the card, pushed it into the bag. She would take it to the lab in the morning.

Maybe the man in the car that she saw earlier was connected.

10

Across town…

"Welcome, welcome. Please sit down…you look tired."

"I'd rather stand now if you don't care," he said looking out the window. "The medicine isn't working…I have memories I can't shake."

"I can change the medication; when did you take it last?"

"Last night, after I started remembering things."

"Let's talk about the memories. Where were you in the memories?"

"I was in my bunk. In the cold building, we were put in. I laid on straw that smelled of urine. My feet. My feet were so cold. Our heads were shaved, and it was cold too. I only had my coat to keep me warm and it didn't cover all my legs and feet. I was so hungry…my stomach hurt. There was a putrid smell in the building…like something burning."

"I wanted to breath fresh air. I looked out the window that had mesh wire across it. The windowpane was broken and some glass missing. There was a slight orange glow in the darkness. The boy in the top bunk was shaking and crying for his mother. He was younger and smaller than me."

"He whimpered and asked if he could get in my bunk to stay warm. I helped him down and stretched my coat around him as much as could. Somehow, we slept."

"So, you put the little boy in your bunk?"

"Yes. I felt so sorry for him. The next morning, getting out of bed, I checked on the little boy, and he was sleeping peacefully. I pulled some loose straw up on him to keep him warm. I tried to open the door to our building but it was locked. I needed a bathroom. I had soiled my clothes again. Some of the other boys had done the same thing and were crying for their parents."

"I pounded on the locked door and a large man in uniform opened it. He said nothing about us changing clothes and just ordered us to get in line for breakfast. A freezing wind was blowing…we all were shivering so bad we could barely stand up. While in line for food, some of the boys just collapsed and were carried away…I never saw them again."

He rubbed his hands together vigorously as if reliving the cold, he had felt years ago. He tapped his shoes rapidly on the floor as if agitated.

"When I got to the head of the food line, I was given a bowl of soup. It was cold. A lady serving the soup handed me two pieces of bread that had green stuff on the edges. She said to eat it…it will make you strong. I ate one and hid the other slice in my shirt for the little boy left in my bunk. We had to eat outside at a table."

"We huddled together to break the wind. When we were done, a big man in uniform came to us and told us to go back to our building and wait for our orders. I hurried back to our building to wake the little boy and get him to eat the bread I saved for him. I shook him gently, then harder. He didn't open his eyes or move. I touched his arm, it was stiff. He was dead. I never knew his name."

Tears formed in his eyes and fell down his shirt. He took a couple of short breaths, covered his eyes with his hands and sobbed.

Several minutes later, he gained his composure and went on. "You have no idea what it was like! The horrible cold and wind. Our clothes soiled, wet and frozen to our skin. I could hear a dog barking. It made me think of the puppy I left behind. I hurried outside and joined the others standing in the snow."

"There was a group of men a few feet from us. They were huddled together trying to keep warm against the gusting wind. I looked for my father but didn't see him in that group. There were two lines for women and older girls further away. Some of the girls were pulled out of the line and hustled to another building. I heard screams…maybe from the girls…I don't know."

"Later that day, I saw my father and other men carrying big blocks of concrete. I hollered at him. He looked up and stopped walking. He called my name. Suddenly, a soldier came up behind him, yelled something at him, then hit the back of his head with the butt of his rifle."

"Was your father hurt bad?"

"He fell to the ground. He tried to get up but the soldier kicked him several times. He tried to get up but couldn't. He was too weak. Two other soldiers dragged him away. I started to cry but the teenage boy next to me said to shut up or they would take me away."

"Did you see your father again?"

"Several weeks later I did. Some of the boys and me were given shovels to scoop snow and ice off the train tracks. When we were told to stop, I saw my father with other men going to their building. They were all dressed in striped shirts and gray pants. My father was tall and the pants were too short for him. He was skinny and pale. He smiled when he saw me. I will never forget that smile."

"Days later, all of us boys were led to a brick pile to carry bricks to another area. The soldier watching us said it was for our new building. We did this for many days and my hands were so sore and bloody. I had no gloves…none of us did. My fingers were numb, and I dropped bricks."

"The man in the long coat yelled at me and threatened I'd go without food if I didn't keep up with the rest of them. Someone called the soldier away. We heard men making some noise, and we stopped and looked ahead. They were chanting something and digging. At least thirty men in a line alongside something like a ditch. From what I could see, it was very deep."

"The teenage boy said the men were digging a trench. There was name-calling by the soldiers and hitting the men with short, thick sticks. Some of the men fell down they were hit so much."

"Those that fell were pushed or kicked into the trench. Then gun fire. One of the soldiers with a gun said the men pushed in the trench were useless and laughed. A soldier in a fancy uniform saw us standing and said to get busy or he would let his dog loose. He was so hateful. He stood close to me as I picked up more bricks. I read his name on his coat."

"What was the man's name?"

"It doesn't matter now but I won't ever forget it! Later, I saw him do terrible things to the men digging the trenches."

"You won't tell me his name?"

"It doesn't matter! He can't hurt anyone ever again."

"But the war is over…you are forty years old now. You could tell me his name."

"For some, the war may be over…but not for me."

"What?"

"I need to go. I'm tired."

"Alright. I will see you next week."

11

"Detective Gillini. Can I help you?"

"Mitch, it's Samantha. Have you got the logs on Kathy Mueller and Sandra Morton?"

"Yeah, and the evidence sheet of the Kramer case."

"Can you meet me at Mike's with everything?"

"Yeah. Give me ten minutes."

Mike's café was crowded, and few noticed the two detectives entering the café. Mitch ordered a beer and a Rueben sandwich from the menu. He handed the log sheets to Samantha who sat ridged in the booth with the menu pushed aside.

"You look like you could tackle a bear. What's up with you?" Mitch asked, puzzled.

"Take a look at this," Samantha said, sliding the envelope across the table. "It was placed in my newspaper last night." Mitch took the envelope and gently opened the flap. He read the message on the card and closed the flap.

"Someone knows you are on the Kramer case."

"And doesn't like it! I'm taking this to the lab and letting Cindy look for prints. Fat chance but worth a try. And another thing. Some guy was parked across the street from my office, looking in my direction on the second floor of the building. He was wearing sunglasses and smoking a cigarette. I didn't think much about it until I found this card."

"I'll get someone to watch your apartment for a day or two. Did you recognize him?" Mitch said.

"Pretty sure the car the guy was sitting in was Levi's, but it wasn't Levi behind the wheel. That guy had broad shoulders and thick forearms." Samantha reached out her hand. "Let me look at the evidence log. I want to see exactly what is on it. This is a copy of it, right? Not the original?" Samantha said, taking the logs from him.

"Yep, I signed it out and went to the copier. I did that with all of the log sheets," Mitch answered, nodding his head as he handed them to Samantha.

"Ok. A witness saw you making the copies, correct?"

"Yes, Sam! What is your problem?" Mitch said in a cutting tone.

"I'm smelling a rat, Mitch. Maybe more than one but I need more proof before I go accusing somebody. I don't want to jump without something solid. I want all documentation wrapped up including witnesses who saw you copy them."

"Okay. Call me when you get home. I'll send a car out after I talk to you. Because you need someone watching the place. Andy isn't there, is he?"

"No, but I'm fine. I don't need someone watching my place, Mitch!"

"How long have you been a cop, Miss Stubborn? You know the statistics as well as I do. Don't override me…I'm sending a car!" Mitch said emphatically. Mitch finished his sandwich, threw money down on the table, and stood up to leave.

As Samantha buttoned her coat, she saw Levi getting off one of the stools at the counter. He stubbed his cigarette out in the ashtray and drew money out of his wallet. He spoke to a man sitting next to him, turned, and left the café. Samantha walked over to where he had sat. She ordered a coffee to go and when no one was looking her way, she picked the cigarette butt out of the ashtray and put it in her coat pocket, grabbed the coffee, turned, and left.

Samantha returned home, checked her mail, and hurried up the stairs to her apartment. She laid the mail on her desk and walked over to the balcony doors. She opened one door and gazed out onto the street. It was clear except for Sunny Days Dry Cleaner's van parked along the curb. It was too early for residents to be home from work.

She closed the door, locked it, and double-checked her apartment door's double locks. All secure. She sat down at her desk and studied the shift logs and evidence log that Mitch had given her. The evidence log looked complete to include the shoes Otto Kramer had worn. The night shift log covering the night Kramer was murdered was accurate.

Both Sgt. Mueller and Officer Morton had signed in and out normal times. The following night shift log, however, showed Sgt. Mueller off sick, Levi Kanter off sick, and Officer Morton taking a personal day.

"I knew it! Somehow those three are connected to this case."

Samantha walked to the entrance door to the police crime lab. Showing her credentials to the receptionist, she was allowed entrance. Seeing Cindy at her computer,

Samantha weaved her way around lab tables filled with microscopes, cyanoacrylate fuming chambers, chromographs, petri dishes and test tubes to Cindy's end of the lab. Not with the least bit friendly voice, Samantha threw out her question to Cindy. "How long would it take to see if there are any prints on this card?"

"Well, hi to you too, Samantha. Is this bite-someone's-head-off day?"

"Sorry, Cindy. Some strange things are happening on this case and I'm trying to piece everything together. This card was in my newspaper…I'm hoping that there are prints on it to help me figure out where it came from and who put it there."

"Well, let's put it in the electronic fingerprint scanner and see. May take thirty to forty-five minutes."

"No problem. I'm going to run down to the evidence room. I'll be back in that length of time."

Samantha took the elevator down to the basement and entered the door marked Evidence Room. Jami came around from the back as Samantha was signing in.

"Jami, I need the box with the evidence collected at the murder scene for Otto Kramer."

"Coming up, Miss O'Malley. Been busy with that case. Officer Kanter was here earlier this morning and was checking the log for the items listed. You guys getting close to finding the killer?"

"No, just doing follow-up stuff. Levi Kanter was here, you say?"

"He didn't stay long. Just looked at the evidence log." Few minutes later, Jami produced the Kramer evidence boxes.

"Two boxes, Miss O'Malley. Take them over to the table if you need to. Initial here before you take them."

Samantha placed her initials on the box tags with the date and time. She took the lid off the box labeled '1' and looked through it for the shoes Otto Kramer was wearing the night he was killed. No shoes. Replacing the lid and pushing the box aside, she removed the lid of the box labeled '2'. Lifting the coat and clothing out she, again, saw no shoes.

"Jami, would you come here a minute. I want you to look in this box."

"What am I looking for?"

"The box lid says coat, shirt, shoes. Where are the shoes?"

"Oh crap! I personally placed them in this box, labeled the lid, numbered it, and placed it on the rack in the back. They aren't in the other box?" Jami asked, frowning.

"No! So, after the autopsy, you were given the shoes to put in evidence, correct?"

"Yeah, I have the slip that Dr. Cullen signed when an intern brought them back here. Look. Here's my initial for receiving them." Jami took the two boxes, replaced them back on the evidence rack, and returned to his desk.

Samantha was already checking the sign-in log again to see who had signed the shoes out. No name. No initials. Nothing. She signed out and left the evidence room and went back upstairs to the crime lab. Reaching Cindy's desk, she read Cindy's facial expression and knew she didn't find any prints.

"Nothing, Samantha. Clean as fresh snow. Perp probably had gloves on. What I did find, which has no bearing on this, was an ash smear on the lower edge of the back of the card. It could be a charcoal smudge or something like that. I'm not sure. I didn't think to look on the back of the card at first," Cindy explained.

"You said ash?" Samantha asked, leaning over Cindy's desk. "What kind of ash?"

Looking puzzled at Samantha's tone, Cindy defensively stated she didn't know. "I can't positively identify it. Maybe charcoal or tobacco ash. There's not enough of it to test. I'm just going by the looks. Here, you look at it." Handing the bagged card back to Samantha, she apologized for not being able to come up with anything.

Samantha agreed there wasn't enough on the corner to make a call as to what it was, but she remembered the man smoking in the parked car the same night the card with the message was in her newspaper.

"Thanks, Cindy. You've been more help than you know."

Samantha left the crime lab with mixed feelings. The missing pair of shoes was high on her mental list of concerns, but the other oddities somehow seemed connected. Somehow, she felt all of them were connected to the Kramer case. Otto Kramer's funeral was mid-afternoon.

She had time to change into something more appropriate and meet Mitch at the funeral home.

Several streets away, Sgt. Kathy Mueller spun the cylinder of her .38 revolver assuring it was fully loaded. Double-checking the safety, she secured it in the holster. Checking the contents of her briefcase, she lowered the top, snapped the closures shut, and locked it before picking it up and heading out her apartment door.

"Ah, crap! Look at that...sprinkles. I bet it's going to pour during the entire funeral and burial," Mueller said when she took her place in the passenger's seat of her partner's car.

"It's overtime...can't be all bad. Who else was assigned funeral duty?" Morton asked.

"There will be four or five around the funeral home and three in the parking lot. All of us are to go to the cemetery. There will be a lot of people attending."

"Are you concerned that someone will be there that you don't want to see or be seen by?"

"No, just cautious," Mueller responded as Morton drove her to the funeral detail meeting.

Once the shift meeting was over, Mueller joined Morton and they drove down Michigan Avenue. Turning left on Clark Street, Mueller directed Morton to turn into the alley behind Kahn's Tailor and Shade Shop. There was time to make a delivery before she needed to show up for funeral duty.

"Good morning, Sergeant!" Yosef Kahn said with a broad smile. Yosef came from Poland to the States a few years after the war. Having no family of his own, he started the tailor shop to support himself and continue the trade of his ancestors in Poland. A slight, impeccably dressed man, he was known for his ready smile and expert workmanship.

Taking the briefcase from Mueller, Yosef hurried down the back hallway to his office. Placing it on his desk, Yosef unlocked it with his key and raised the lid to see the contents.

"My, my. These skins are perfect. They are wide and clear of blemishes," Yosef said, examining the items. "I will dye these a pretty shade of blue. I believe I can make one large one and one small one from these skins. I have a customer who is wanting one for her entryway table. If it turns out nice, it will be perfect for her. Oh, I am so pleased with these. All my customers have been pleased with the shades."

He clasped his hands together as if in prayer. Lifting the items from the briefcase, Kahn laid them on a metal rack display. He walked back to the table, closed the briefcase, and locked it. Turning from the table, he shook hands with Mueller and walked her to the door. "When will you have more?" He asked in a whisper.

"I want more as soon as you can get them," Kahn demanded.

Mueller just stared at the door for a few moments, opened it, and walked back to Morton's car.

"Well, how did it go?"

"He wants more. He always wants more."

12

The funeral was short and non-eventful. The funeral home was full of people, leaving many to stand in the vestibule. Samantha stood inside by the exit door. She noticed Mrs. Kramer dressed in an all-black dress made of heavy material. No jewelry. On her head was a black hat with a black course knit netting that covered her face making it almost invisible.

Glancing over the large room filled with people, she saw Mueller. *That made sense*, Samantha thought. She was the one who responded to the call and spent time questioning Mrs. Kramer. She's just showing respect.

Mrs. Kramer spoke to no one when the last hymn was sung and the minister said the final prayer. She followed the casket out of the funeral home though her head was bowed, and again, Samantha could not see her face.

Mitch stood among the trees several yards from the funeral home's parking lot. Rain peppered down the back of his neck and on his jacket. The trees had leafed out with the warmth of spring and gentle rains but didn't conceal him as much as he liked. He moved to an impenetrable brushy area and crouched down to avoid being seen.

As he watched the mourners coming out of the funeral home, he kept thinking about Samantha. She hadn't called like she said she would, and he hadn't seen her until now at the funeral. Some of the mourners he recognized as business owners, others he didn't know. Observing people returning to their cars, he spotted Mueller walking down a line of cars. She stopped and talked with a man noticeably shorter than herself.

Mitch could tell the man was upset about something. Mueller put her hands on his shoulders. Mitch could not interpret what she was saying, but whatever it was, it didn't help to calm the man down. Mueller spoke loud enough to draw looks from others, though no one stopped. Just then, Officer Levi Kanter jogged up to where the conversation was continuing and got between the two of them. He took the man by the arm and led him away from Mueller.

"What the hell?" Mitch thought out loud. He stood up to get a better look. Mueller turned sharply and went in the opposite direction. Levi and the man disappeared in the crowd.

Turning back toward the hearse, he saw Mrs. Kramer being helped into the back seat of the hearse by one of the pallbearers. Cars started coming his way, so he crouched down in the thicket to avoid being seen. Looking back at the funeral home's entrance, he saw Samantha coming out. She walked to her car slowly and looked around as if looking for somebody.

She glanced in Mitch's way as the last car was leaving the parking lot. He stood up, and she nodded to him.

"Did you forget something, lady?" Mitch asked when they were back at her office.

"What do you mean?"

"You were to call me so I would know you were okay when you got home."

"Mitch, I locked all the doors and got busy with the reports. I guess I felt safe and secure and totally forgot to call."

"Well, you had me concerned. I didn't see you at the funeral until you were headed for your car."

"All my fault, I'm sorry," Samantha said, apologetic.

"Alright, I'm going home. I'll talk to Steve and make sure he's watching the warehouse tonight. I'll give him both our phone numbers if he needs to call."

"Hopefully, I'm meeting Andy tonight for dinner. Why don't you join us?"

"Maybe. Give me a call, and if I don't answer…the answer is no. Oh, don't bother to keep calling either."

"Someone waiting for you?" Samantha asked with a huge grin.

"There may be two waiting for me!" Mitch retorted jokingly.

"You think you can handle two women, Mitch?" Heather kiddingly asked as she walked up to the group. She was always glad to see Mitch and hearing the conversation.

"The question is can two women handle me?" Mitch said as he walked to the door.

"That's not good for the heart, Mitch," Heather hollered.

"Hey, if they die…they die!" Chuckling, Mitch walked through the door.

"That guy is so funny," Heather said shaking her head and laughing. "I wish he would find someone. He does nothing but work. I think he's married to it! Do you think he'll meet you and Andy?"

"Who knows. He's not known for turning down food!" Samantha answered with a smile.

"Speaking of Andy, I'm going to try and reach him again." Samantha picked up the phone and called Andy's office.

"Hello? Courson Construction."

"Hey, Jean. Any sign of Andy yet?"

"He left a good fifteen minutes ago, Samantha. Didn't say where he was going, and I never thought to ask, but I did give him your message."

"That's okay. He's probably on his way to my place. Do have a good evening, Jean." Samantha hung the phone up.

"How are things going with the case? You look frazzled," Heather said with concern.

"Actually, it's moving along rather well. Things are falling into place. But you would not believe what Mitch and I found at the old warehouse. Guess there are no messages for me?" Samantha asked as she checked so files in the file cabinet.

"Nope, it's been a quiet day, and I'm glad. I almost have all of your notes typed up."

"Okay, good. I'm going upstairs to soak in the tub. Arthur will need out too. Hey, if you're done, go on home. Transfer the phone to mine upstairs."

Samantha moved her phone into the bathroom while hot water filled her tub. She went into the living room to find Arthur who was waiting at the balcony door.

"Okay, big guy, I'll let you out." Arthur sauntered out and hopped onto the wicker chair he loved to sleep in.

Samantha looked down at the street and everything looked normal…only the Sunny Days Dry Cleaner's van was still parked down the street. She locked the balcony doors, double-checked her front door, and returned to the bathroom.

She sunk down in the tub, letting the perfumed bubbles cover her. The steam melted her stress and soothed the aches in her neck. For a while, no questions cluttered her mind. Peace and tranquility consumed her. Then she heard her front door open.

"Hey, babe. I'm here," Andy announced.

"Okay. Give me a couple of minutes." Samantha got out of the tub, wrapped a towel around her and walked into the living room.

"You are beautiful wrapped in a towel," Andy said looking at her.

"Really? Let me get my sandals on, and I'm ready to go," Samantha said, laughing.

"I dare you. I'll give a year's income if you go like that." Andy pulled the towel away as he grabbed her. He held her tight and kissed her hard.

"We could have dessert first, you know."

Giggling, Samantha escaped his arms and walked toward her bedroom. "You better know a good bondsman then I."

"Yes! I love it!" Andy said as he watched her leave.

"Hey, where are we going? I need to know what to wear."

"I have reservations at Joe's Seafood on Grand Ave."

Ten minutes later, she appeared in a black, backless dress. The front bared her midriff and drew attention to the curve of her breasts.

"Ah, yes. It's going to be a special night. I can tell!" Andy said when he saw her.

They were seated at a table for two with a beautiful view of Lake Michigan. The neon sign for the Drake Hotel was framed on the side of the room by sheer drapes. A bottle of wine was immediately brought to the table.

"The scenery is beautiful, Andy. The moon makes the lake glisten."

"I thought you would like it. So how is the case going?"

"Andy, that warehouse plays a big part in it. Someone is constructing a mock concentration camp death chamber in it. I'm talking rooms equipped with shower heads, piping that may contain some kind of fluid. Spigots placed in the shower heads. Someone is on a mission to recreate the death chambers. It gave me the chills."

Samantha leaned back in her chair as if the memory took her strength away. She stared out the window in hopes the memory would vanish and be replaced by the view she saw.

"Hey, it's okay, Sam. Honey, do you want to talk about something else? I'm sorry I asked. I had no idea." Andy took her hand and held it.

The waiter brought menus and quietly left.

"It's okay. It's just mystifying. My brain is consumed by it. Mitch and I found large cylinders and have no idea what could be in them. A detective friend of Mitch's is going to spend some nights outside to see if anyone shows up. The parking lot was empty when we were there. Maybe someone is working in it at night."

The waiter reappeared. "Are you ready to order?"

The rest of the evening was dedicated to small talk, their meals, and where Andy had to go next. They left the restaurant and went to a small club or drinks. It was well past 1 a.m. when they returned to her apartment. As they climbed the stairs, Samantha noticed one of her business cards laying on a step. She wondered why it was there, knowing it wasn't when they left. She picked it up and put it in her purse. Climbing to the top, Samantha noticed a light under the door. She stopped.

"Did you leave a light on when we left?" Andy asked.

Putting a finger to her lips, she shook her head. She retrieved her gun from her purse and listened for movement or voices on the inside. Believing no one was inside, she pushed the unlatched door all the way open. Arthur did not come to her which was out of character for him.

Lamps turned over; drawers opened with contents scattered on the floor, pillows and couch cushions removed. This was the scene that greeted Samantha. "What are they after and why?" She asked, mostly to herself.

"I'm calling the police," Andy said as he walked toward her desk.

"Don't touch anything, Andy!" Using his handkerchief to remove the receiver, he dialed the number.

Samantha started looking for Arthur. He finally came out from under her bed when he saw her walk into the bedroom. She picked him up and returned to the living room.

"They are on their way," Andy said solemnly.

Samantha looked at her desk and the shuffled, scattered papers that were not in the order she had left them when they left for dinner. She took a pencil and pulled the desk drawers open one by one by the antique drawer pulls looking for the reports she had on the Kramer murder case. The file was gone. So were the lab reports.

"Everything's gone! They took all the damn reports and Kramer files! I want to go down to the office and see if it was broken into," Samantha said with a shaky voice.

"Hang on. You aren't going alone," Andy said, following her down the steps.

"The door is still locked." She reached into her purse for her keys and opened the door. She used a key to flip on the light to avoid touching it. Everything looked normal. She walked to the file cabinets and found them locked.

"I want the door, desk, and file cabinet dusted for prints," she stated out loud. She took a second look around the room, left the door unlocked, and they returned upstairs. A rap on the apartment door sounded.

"Police!" Sgt. Mueller and Officer Morton entered and looked at Samantha.

"I'm Sgt. Mueller and this is Officer Morton," Mueller said to Samantha and Andy.

"Most excitement we've had all night, Miss O'Malley," Mueller said smiling but trying to look serious.

"There's nothing amusing about this."

"Who are you, Sir?" Mueller asked looking at Andy.

"A friend of Samantha's."

"Your full name, Sir," Mueller said.

"Not necessary, Sergeant! He's not involved. He was with me," Samantha said sternly.

Turning to Samantha, Mueller said, "Tell me what happened."

Samantha retold the events of the evening and night to her.

"I want fingerprints taken on my office door, desk, and file cabinet."

"That's being done by an officer now, Ma'am," Mueller stated.

Another officer Samantha didn't know entered the apartment with a fingerprint kit.

"Dust everything, Randy. Especially the desk," Mueller said.

Samantha watched Mueller, who had followed him, looking at the scattered papers on her desk and floor.

"You are here to find the culprit…not read the stuff on my desk!" Samantha said, agitated.

Mueller slowly moved to the side still looking at the papers.

"Something there you want, Sergeant?" Samantha asked again watching her closely.

Mueller walked away and made some notes, not responding. Andy walked over to Samantha and whispered that the other female officer went into Samantha's bedroom. Samantha quietly walked to the bedroom doorway and saw Morton opening her dresser drawers. She closed each drawer quietly after looking through the contents. When she had looked through all of them, she walked to the closet and opened the door.

Samantha came quietly into the room and stood at the foot of the bed watching Morton, who was going through the clothes on hangers, then squatted down going through shoe boxes on the floor.

"Hey, Morton, is this what they taught you in the academy? Rummaging through drawers and shoe boxes? Is it a new technique in finding clues to a break-in?" Samantha whispered, standing over Morton.

Morton jumped up not realizing Samantha was in the room or standing behind her. She looked at Samantha with a red face. "Just thought maybe…well, maybe something was left behind by whoever did this."

"In shoe boxes? Really, Morton?"

"The drawers and boxes were neat and orderly. Now they are a mess. Trying to make it look like the burglar was in the bedroom, Morton? Get out of here!" Samantha said loudly.

Morton hurried from the bedroom and looked at Mueller who glared at her but said nothing.

"I think I have everything, Sergeant," Randy said as he put his brushes and roll of fingerprint tape back in the fingerprint case.

"Someone will get back with you, Miss O'Malley. I have your business card. Good night," Mueller said in a matter-of-fact tone.

Samantha walked out onto the balcony not returning a comment. She walked to the banister to watch the three return to their patrol cars. Andy closed and locked the door behind them and walked to the balcony.

"I wonder how Mueller got my business card. I never gave her one…did you?" She said to Andy.

"No."

“I have a very good idea who broke in! I had a stack of business cards along the side of the desk. They are scattered around and the one on the steps I saw tells me a lot.”

The two of them took a seat on the wicker couch on the dark balcony. Samantha looked out on the street and watched the Sunny Days van pull away from the curb toward Lake Shore Drive.

“Well, ain’t that peculiar? That van driver didn’t turn the van lights on,” she said with a smirk.

The wheels in her head were turning.

“What about the missing files, Sam?” Andy asked thinking about the documented evidence lost.

“Heather makes copies of everything,” Samantha answered still watching the van. “The original copies that Mitch got me were locked in the office filing cabinet. I only had copies of those in my desk. There is a special imprint that’s hardly noticeable on the copies in my desk. It’s a good way to tell if someone has stolen them, which copies, and where they were from if they turn up in someone else’s possession.”

“Brilliant!” Andy said smiling at her.

“My dad did that with copies of paperwork he had on cases when he was a cop. Often comes in handy later in court.”

They went back into the apartment and Andy fixed them a drink as Samantha straightened her desktop hoping it would calm her. She would tend to the closet and drawers in the morning.

She was silent when she prepared for bed and Andy didn’t push her to talk. He had an idea what she was thinking. In bed, Andy covered her with his arm and fell asleep. Samantha, feeling safe, lay awake wondering if her suspicions were true.

Mitch had heard the dispatcher send units to Samantha's apartment for the break-in and responded on his own. He parked at the end of the block, cut the engine, turned the lights off and watched who responded. Fifty minutes later, he watched as the three officers left. Mitch could see that Andy was going to stay with Samantha. He was about to leave when he saw brake lights come on the Sunny Days van across the street.

Watching it pull away from the curb with no headlights, he decided to follow it thinking that was weird. Traffic was minimal, so he stayed his distance as the van turned onto Lake Shore Drive. When the lights on the van came on, he pulled back another car length and let other vehicles get between the van and his car.

He watched the van turn onto Clark Street, turn off the lights, and pull in the alley. It stopped at the dock to the old warehouse. Sitting for a few minutes, two men got out. One…was Levi Kanter. Several minutes later, they returned and sat in the van, talking. The lights came on and they left.

13

Across town, early the next morning.

A knock on the door.

"Goodness! I haven't even got the coffee started," the therapist said, opening the door. "Would you like some when it's ready?"

"That would be okay," the man said as he walked to the large window. "I like looking out the window. Everything is fresh in the morning. People look happy. Their lives are full of good things, good memories. Not like mine."

"We are working on bringing that back for you. You have to work harder on that. What do you want to talk about today?"

"A memory that woke me up early this morning. It keeps replaying in my mind. That's why I'm here."

"Tell me about it. I'll pour our coffee."

"One day, it rained all day. All of us boys played games on the floor in our building with small rocks we picked up outside. It was a dark, rainy day, and we didn't have to carry bricks. By late afternoon, the rain stopped. We were having a good time when we heard a loud motor outside, close to our building."

"We went to the windows and watched the driver of a large truck get out and talk to the evil soldier that always stayed around our building. I don't know where the truck came from. After they talked a while, the truck driver went back to the side of the truck and opened a sliding door. A man inside came to the opening and stood looking out."

"Another man walked up. He was one of us. He wore stripped pants and a gray shirt. He pushed a long-bed cart alongside the open door. When I looked inside the truck, I saw a heap of bodies. They were dead bodies. The man outside of the truck with the cart was told to move the cart closer to the truck bed."

"The man inside began to push the bodies out of the truck onto the cart. Bodies just kept coming. It made me sick to watch the bodies fall but I couldn't look away. The man outside stacked the bodies up like he was stacking boxes. When the cart was overflowing with skeleton-like bodies, it was pulled away by men from the camp to the deep trench I saw my father and other men digging."

"Three other men showed up in long coats and high black boots. They pulled the bodies off the cart and threw them in the trench."

"This routine went on a long time. When the truck was empty, the driver got back in and backed out. When the truck was out of sight, the men with the long coats poured some chemical over the bodies in the trench and lit a torch. They burned the bodies. BURNED THEM! Can you imagine seeing that?"

He paced back and forth by the window. Glancing out now and then as if he might see the scene in his mind for real.

"Later that night, a bulldozer drove up and pushed dirt on what was left of the bodies and filled the trench. Men with rakes stood on the dirt and smoothed it all out making it look like nothing was under it. This didn't end with just one truck. Oh my God! Truck after truck came and unloaded dead bodies. The carts that bodies were put on went to other trenches that had been dug like the one I saw my father at."

"Some of those bodies were burned and buried…others just burned. The stench filled our building and we vomited until some of the younger boys passed out and laid on the cold floor."

"The teenage boy that was housed with us said they came from Chelmo, his family's town. The Nazis told the residents in Chelmo that they were being taken to Germany by truck to work. The residents were overjoyed…they would be laborers and live. They followed the orders given by the Nazi soldiers to bathe and have their clothes disinfected prior to leaving their village."

"As soon as the trucks were full, the doors were locked and CO was piped into the truck bed. The gas asphyxiated all of them in the trucks. The teenage boy said they all died and were buried in mass graves outside of their village."

"Were all the people around Chelmno treated this way?"

"That's what I was told. When suspicion about it was becoming noticed, the rest were trucked to Auschwitz, where we were, and dumped in trenches and burned. Thousands of them. Truck after truck came all through the night. My father and the other men worked around the clock. I can see them…I can…"

"You are trembling. Please come sit down. I will get you some water."

"It's the odor I can still smell. The smell of burning flesh filled the camp. The smoke from the chimneys filled the air. We couldn't get away from it. There was no fresh air in the whole camp. It lasted for days. Burning and covering with dirt didn't help. The smell lingered," he said as he sat down in the leather chair.

"Do you want to rest for a while?"

"No. My head is throbbing with these memories! They haunt me in the night. I see the soldiers laying some of the bodies out on the frozen ground. They all carried pliers and would pry the mouths of the dead people open and extract gold teeth. I see the soldiers laughing and counting the fragments of gold they each had."

"They had a lottery on who could pull out the most teeth with gold. They pocketed the gold. I can see the Nazi officer that laughed the loudest. He turned and faced our building."

"So you see his face in your memories, and you remember him. Who was he? What was his name?"

"I told you it doesn't matter anymore! He can't hurt anybody ever again."

"Why do you say that? Do you know him? Have you seen him?"

"YES! I have seen him! I know where he worked! I heard his heinous laugh! I remember seeing his boots and his ugly coat he wore when I had no coat and no boots! Don't you see…he is here!"

"Here? You have seen him here in Chicago?"

"Oh yes. I have seen him here in Chicago. I know he is the same person that was in our camp."

“You must go to the FBI and tell them. He must have escaped from Germany. He’s a war criminal. I will go with you if you want me to.”

“No, there is more about him that you don’t know…that I haven’t told you…my head hurts so bad. I can’t stand the pain and the memories! I remember the women. The work they were forced to do. The screams at night from their building and the building they called a hospital…it all rushes in my head…the pain…I can’t stand the pain!”

He sobbed until he was drained of strength and fell back in the chair and slept.

14

Andy could hear the shower running and walked into the kitchen. He opened the refrigerator and removed two ham steaks and four eggs. Samantha walked out of the bedroom, pulling the ties of her floor length robe together, her wet hair wrapped in a towel turban style.

"Ten minutes and breakfast will be served," Andy announced.

"Smells good, Andy. Sorry, I overslept. I couldn't get to sleep right away last night. I want to get with the cop who was supposed to be watching the apartment yesterday and find out where in the hell he was! This shouldn't have happened!" Samantha walked to her desk to call Mitch just as someone knocked on the door.

"Hey, everyone up?" Mitch said, standing in the doorway and knowing what was coming just by the look on Samantha's face as she opened the door.

"Where in the hell was my guardian, Mitch? Andy and I went out and you were supposed to have someone here! Go on, you're good for excuses! Let's hear it!"

"Calm down. There was a pile-up on the expressway with several fatalities. He called me and told me he was responding per his captain's orders. When he was done there, he came back and stayed until five a.m. The sun was coming up and he didn't want to be seen by your neighbors. He walked around your building a few times and made checks on cars park on the street. He did the best he could."

Samantha, with arms crossed, wasn't satisfied. "They took my reports…my files on the Kramer case. Damn it! They went through my drawers in the bedroom and that incompetent partner of Mueller's went through the shoeboxes in my closet! My shoeboxes! What the hell!"

Mitch cleared his throat and continued to try to justify the hours there was no coverage for her.

Pointless. He knew Samantha…the perfectionist, the organized one, the one that was beautiful even when she was angry, the woman he still adored. He looked at Andy when Samantha turned her back to him and threw his hands up.

"Sam, I don't run the department. You know how it works," Mitch said defensively.

Samantha walked to the balcony doors and stared out at nothing in particular, remaining silent.

"So, Mitch, have you had breakfast? Plenty here," Andy asked hoping to break the tension that consumed the room.

"Take a seat, Mitch. I'm done ranting," Samantha said, turning to face the men.

Andy got another ham steak out of the refrigerator and three more eggs. He scrambled the eggs in silence not looking for approval from Samantha. Mitch walked over to Samantha to tell her what he had seen last night.

"Sam, I heard the radio call to your address and responded. I was parked at the end of the block and saw Mueller and the other two go in and out of your building. I also saw Sunny Days' dry-cleaning van pull onto Oak Street with no lights and turn onto Lake Shore Drive. I followed them to Clark Street and watched them take the alley to the back of the warehouse. Two men were in the van. I watched them get out. Levi Kanter was one of them."

"Any idea who the other one was?" Samantha asked quietly.

"No…never saw him before. Big, burly type. Didn't see his face. Couldn't tell much more…too dark."

"That description is like the man I saw outside my apartment in what looked like Levi's car. Have you seen your friend, Steve, yet this morning? I'm anxious to see what he saw."

"That's next. I know he is off shift at 7:00 this morning. You and I will meet with him after breakfast. But I don't think he did much, except watch, this time," Mitch said.

Andy called the two to the table and the three of them enjoyed the food while making small talk. Samantha was first to get up and head for the bedroom to change. She dried her hair, put jeans and a sweatshirt on. Touched up her mascara and lipstick. She was slipping on her loafers when she heard Mitch telling Andy thanks for breakfast and opening the apartment door.

Stumbling around the bed and limping out to the living room with just one shoe on, she caught Mitch going down the stairs.

"Hey, wait a minute…you aren't going without me! Give me two minutes!" Mitch, grinning, sat down on one of the steps and waited for her. She grabbed her other shoe, kissed Andy, and flew out of the room, slamming the door behind her.

"I wasn't going to leave without you. Wanted to warm up the car…temperature dropped last night. Pretty chilly for May," Mitch said still grinning when they were on their way to Joliet.

"Hi, Mitch and Miss O'Malley," Steve Jordon greeted the two when Mitch pulled his car alongside of his in a restaurant parking lot. The threesome went into the restaurant and ordered coffee.

"I didn't push my luck this time. I got the license number on the van and pictures of the two guys…even one showing them entering the warehouse and one exiting later. They never turned on any lights that I could see and were only there twenty-seven minutes. They didn't bring anything out with them."

"The big, stocky guy drove. He took the passenger home and returned the van to the dry-cleaning parking lot. He got out, locked it, and got into his own car. I got the info from his personal car too. Here's the info on it." Steve Jordon tore a page out of his note pad with the vehicle information and handed it to Samantha.

"I'll get the film developed today and be back tonight. Maybe try to get in before they show up…if they show up. Gotta go. Nice meeting you, Miss O'Malley." Jordon left Mitch and Samantha sitting in the booth reviewing the new clues on the piece of paper.

"I'm not shocked that Levi is involved with this. I suspected him almost from the start," Samantha said as she stirred her coffee.

"Yeah, doesn't look good for him. But why? He's a good officer. No family as far as I know. Been in Chicago most of his life. Not married. I just don't get it. Only thing

I've noticed, he doesn't do anything after work…at least I didn't think so."

"Remember I said I saw Mueller sitting in his car the day of the chemical spill? I wondered then why she was in there and now I'm wondering if she is connected to this. The two of them and Morton were all off shift around the time of Kramer's murder. Coincidence?" Samantha reminisced.

"I don't know…maybe," Mitch said, standing up. "I'll get you back home. Call me at noon."

"Yeah, I'll do that. I want to get into his house if at all possible," Samantha said staring off into space. "That may tell us what we want to know. Do you know anyone in personnel? I'd like to see Kanter's file and the background on him," Samantha said as she stood up looking at her watch.

"You don't ask for much, lady! Why don't you ask me to break into Fort Knox? That's all confidential, Sam. Not just anybody can get access to that information. Don't bet on me getting anything there, but I'll do what I can," Mitch said standing outside of the car.

"Remember we have the lead in this investigation and access to whatever we need. The police department has to provide us with everything we ask for."

"Yeah, but that's going…oh hell, what's the use! I had hoped to retire from the department…not get kicked out!"

Samantha smiled at Mitch when he quit mumbling. She wouldn't do anything that would get him fired. They reached her building and Samantha got out.

"Don't forget to call me at noon," Mitch hollered as she shut her door.

"Hi, Heather, anything going on?" Samantha asked when she entered her office.

"Here's the phone call notes. The phone won't quit ringing. I'm going to have an elephant ear before this is over. Seems the word is out that you are handling the Kramer case. The mayor and Chief Van Watson were on TV this morning. The Tribune wants an interview with you, and a representative from Channel 2 wants you to call him back. No reason given," Heather said, pushing the notes toward her.

"Okay. I've got to get some groceries and let Arthur out. I'll tackle these when I get back," she said, picking up the notes. "Can I bring you something back for lunch?"

"Oh, sure...I'd like a thick prime rib, medium rare, smothered in sauteed mushrooms, baked potato with double butter and sour cream, tossed salad with honey mustard dressing, two French bread slices, and a white Russian...make that a double white Russian," Heather rattled off as if rehearsed.

"Is that on your diet?"

"Today, yes. I'm earning my pay for sure!" Heather smiled and returned to her typing.

Samantha, grinning, shook her head and hurried upstairs to grab the grocery list off the refrigerator door. Arthur purred at her feet and followed her to the balcony doors. "I'm late, aren't I, big guy?" She opened the door for him and watched as he hurried through and jumped up on the wicker couch.

Traffic was heavy when she turned on State Street. Glancing in her rear-view mirror, she noticed a car staying close behind her. She switched to the left lane when she could squeeze in and kept an eye on the mirror. Reaching the grocery store, she waited to see if the car followed her into the parking lot.

Not seeing the car, she got out and entered the grocery store. After a twenty-minute shopping trip, she stood as the automatic exit doors opened and saw the mystery car straight in front of her. Two men sat in the front seat. She ignored the car and went straight to hers. After placing the bags in the trunk, she walked over to the car with the two men inside.

The window was down on the passenger side. She walked up to it silently.

"Dixon, what the hell are you doing following me?"

Shocked, Matt Dixon stumbled for words. "Hey. Oh, hi, O'Malley."

"Dixon, what are you and Carter following me for?"

"Just following orders, Samantha. The chief wanted us to keep an eye on you. We didn't ask for this detail. Didn't want to do it…just ordered to," Dixon said apologetically.

She slapped the top of their car and went back to her own. She looked at her watch. 12 noon straight up. Instead of going back to the office, she steered the car back to Michigan Avenue and parked outside of the back door to Bandera, the chief's favorite lunch hangout.

Stomping through the kitchen to the surprised look on the cooks' faces, Samantha proceeded through the dining area to where the chief was sitting with the city mayor and two other district lieutenants. Seeing her approach, Chief Van Watson put down his fork and looked at her.

"Why are you having me followed?" She asked through her teeth, looking directly at the chief.

"What are you talking about, Miss O'Malley?"

"Carter and Dixon followed me all the way down State Street and even to the grocery store. I asked them why and they said you ordered them to follow me! Now, tell me why!"

"There must have been a miscommunication. Can we talk about this later?" The chief said nonchalantly.

"No, I want to know now! I don't have time to keep looking over my shoulder, and you should have better use of your officers."

"Well." Wiping his mouth with the linen napkin and taking a sip of water, the chief continued.

"I had not heard from you since our initial phone conversation when I instructed you to keep me in the loop on this case," the chief said.

"When I have something substantial and solid, Chief, I will fill you in. At this time, I don't, and being followed all over the city is not speeding things along. I want you to get the hell off my back!" Samantha said sternly and loud enough for the neighboring diners to look at the chief's table.

"Miss O'Malley, you are talking to the chief of police! My goodness, show some respect," the mayor quietly chastised Samantha.

"I apologize, Mayor…you are correct. I'll rephrase. Get the fuck off my back, Chief!" Samantha straightened up, turned, and left the restaurant the way she came in, leaving the other diners watching her with dropped jaws.

Returning to her office, she called Mitch. As soon as Mitch picked up the phone, she said, "I'm at my office going over some files. Hope I'm not making you late for anything."

"Nope. Just going to stay in hiding until I think I can go to personnel without being noticed. Then I'll be writing my obituary," Mitch answered sarcastically.

Samantha laughed and assured him he would be fine. The task was right up his alley.

"Samantha, all the files that were taken the other night have been copied from the files in the locked file cabinet. I think I have them in order," Heather said, turning away from her typewriter. "Oh, Mrs. Henricks stopped in asking how you were. She said she's a light sleeper, but never heard anyone enter before the police came. She wished now she had. That maybe she could have called the police and they could have caught whoever did this."

"Not her fault. I'll talk with her before I go up to my apartment." Just then, the phone rang.

"Yes, one moment…I'll transfer you to her desk." Heather pushed the transfer button. "It's the chief's secretary. She said the chief is on the warpath. He wants you in his office now. He s been yelling at everyone all afternoon."

Samantha took the call at her desk. "Yes, Chief."

"I'd like you to come to my office, Miss O'Malley. Right now would be in your best interest."

"What's this about?" Samantha calmly asked.

"I want to go over protocol and your conduct in the restaurant earlier."

"Let me see what I have free." She laid the receiver down, rustled several papers loud enough to hurt his ear, stopped and picked up the phone. "I have later this afternoon free. Looks like twenty free minutes, Chief." Samantha winked at Heather who saw what she did.

"1630 then. Be here!"

"Do I say 50 Hail Marys before I arrive?" Samantha asked knowing the chief couldn't see her smiling. "Hello…Chief…are you there? I'll be damned…he hung up on me!"

At 4:00, Samantha left her office and drove to the police department. Before she left, she left a coded message on Mitch's radio so he would know where she was going and what time. Taking the elevator up to the chief's office, she took a deep breath and opened the receptionist door.

"Hi, Katrina. Has he simmered down any?" Samantha whispered as she seated herself in a chair.

"Not at all. Saw him pacing back and forth earlier. Also heard you sorta made him look like an ass while he was having lunch with the mayor," Katrina said smiling.

"He had it coming!"

Katrina's phone buzzed. "Go on in, Samantha, and good luck!" Samantha walked into the chief's office and stood facing the chief and leaving the door partly open.

"Have a seat, Miss O'Malley," the chief said not looking at her.

"I'm fine standing, Sir. What is it you want to say?" Samantha said.

"You attempted to make an ass out of me in public and in front of the mayor and my lieutenants. You owe me an apology!"

"For what? As I see it, you owe me one. I'm not a rookie. You know the way I work in solving crimes. Why have bloodhounds following me all over? Sorry, can't apologize. I meant what I said."

Chief Van Watson stood and walked to the other side of his desk and looked straight into Samantha's eyes. In a threatening tone, he said, "If you ever do that again I'll…"

"Hang on. I want the door open wide so there is a witness to what you are going to say."

Samantha opened the door wide so Katrina, sitting at her desk, had total view of the chief and Samantha and could hear everything he said. "Okay, go ahead…tell me what you will do."

"O'Malley, I'll have your license and your reputation! I'll drag your name through the mud. When I get done, the only cases you will get are dead-beats and cheating spouses!"

"Is that it, Chief? Time's up," Samantha asked as she turned to walk out of his office.

"One more thing, O'Malley, Katrina isn't going to hear a thing…are you, Katrina?" The chief said with a glare looking through the doorway at Katrina.

15

Samantha kicked off her shoes as she sifted through her mail. Her phone buzzed indicating a call from her office downstairs.

"Yes, Heather."

"A man on line 1 by the name of Steve Jordon wants to talk to you."

"Sure. Transfer the call."

"Hello, Steve."

"Samantha, am I interrupting anything?"

"Only solving this Kramer case," she said with a chuckle. "What's going on?"

"I'm in Skokie and know this is a late request, but would you join me for dinner this evening?"

"Ah…well, I don't have anything scheduled his evening. Sure…guess so," she said puzzled that he would be calling her.

"I'll pick you up at 7:00. See you then." Jordon's phone went dead.

She replaced the receiver gently. She knew he had her number, Mitch had given it to him days earlier. *Maybe he has some new information on the warehouse*, she thought. She decided to take a quick shower and dress casually.

Jordon hadn't said where they were going. She would also call Mitch.

"Hello," Mitch answered his phone just as Samantha was ready to hang up.

"Mitch, have you talked with Steve Jordon lately?"

"No, figured nothing new at the warehouse so no reason to call me or you. Why?"

"Well, he's taking me to dinner. We just hung up. I wonder if something has happened, or he's been made," Samantha stated in a questioning tone.

"Jordon made? Are you kidding?" Mitch laughed. "His nickname on the force is Ghost. He's never been made on any stakeout."

"Okay, just seemed strange. I only met him that one time."

"Just go and enjoy the food for Pete's sake. He's a nice guy."

"Yeah. See ya." Samantha hung up not feeling any more comfortable.

Samantha was looking out the balcony doors when she saw a black Porsche pull in along the curb by her house. Steve looked up at her apartment and waved as he closed the car door. She met him at the building entrance and together they walked back to his car.

Fastening her seat belt, Steve asked if Mike's was okay. "Sure, if that suits you." She was still thinking he was going to drop a bombshell on her and dinner was a way to soften the blow. "Steve, how did you know where I lived?"

"I wondered when you were going to get around to asking me that. It's no big secret. Mitch and I were comparing notes about the warehouse and the subject of you came up. I just came out and asked all the pertinent questions, and Mitch was an open book. He was very professional, Samantha. Nothing personal. He's very fond of you if you didn't know and trusts you with his life," Steve said hoping to get her to relax.

Samantha watched kids playing in the park as they headed toward Mike's. She remained silent until they parked and got out. They ordered spaghetti and garlic sticks and Steve explained he knew some people in Skokie he wanted to see.

"Friend or foe?" Samantha asked with a smile.

"Friend mostly. A couple of the families are survivors of the Holocaust, and the others are Jews that migrated to the states before the war broke out. I wanted to know if they knew of the Kramers or Himmey Miller. Struck out. None of them had heard of either name. I thought maybe they could shed some light on Otto Kramer's murder. Those that I asked said they only knew what they read in the Tribune."

"Interesting, Steve. When Mitch and I interviewed Mrs. Kramer, I felt she was hiding something. I want a closer look at her."

The waiter reappeared and offered a drink menu. Steve ordered two glasses of red wine.

"Well, I do know that the German population was pretty high before WWII but has been reduced over the last couple of decades. There is a larger Jewish community there now."

"So, you don't have a personal connection to Skokie, right?" Samantha asked between sips.

"No…not really. I grew up in southern Indiana and went to college in Carbondale, IL. I attended the police academy, like you, and decided to stay in Chicago. Like you."

"Sounds like Mitch didn't leave much out concerning my biography. What else did he tell you?" She asked with a smile.

"Just that he was pretty ornery as a kid and gave you a rough time." Laughter followed from both of them.

"So, why did you want to be a cop? I could see you as a fashion designer, a professional model, or a corporate executive…anything but a cop."

"I really started out thinking I wanted to be an attorney and studied criminal law, but Mitch talked me into going to the academy, and I changed my mind. It paid off. I found being a cop was rewarding most of the time. When I tested to move up in the ranks, I was either slapped down or totally ignored and figured out I was going nowhere."

"I got my master's out east. I moved back here, got my detective's license, and here I am," Samantha said, summarizing her work history.

"Mitch said you have done well with cases the PD hasn't been able to solve. The murder on Lake Shore Drive made the headlines, but your picture in the Tribune didn't do you justice."

"I made more enemies than friends on that case. Chief Van Watson thought it was a huge black mark against his department because I solved it and got all the attention. The city council and the mayor raked the chief over the coals and said nothing to me…which was fine. I was paid well anyway. The family of the victim that hired me was wealthy."

"The Kramer case seems to have a lot of twists and turns. The warehouse seems totally abandoned and just a dilapidated building. What piqued your interest in the case?" Jordon asked. Samantha looked down at her drink and didn't respond.

"Hey, let's drop the business talk! A friend of mine owns a piano bar over on Rush Street. Would you like to go there and have a couple of drinks? I promise to get you home before curfew." They both laughed.

The piano bar was crowded but they found a cozy table for two in a far corner. Steve ordered drinks.

"Samantha, I'm usually not this forward with women, but I have to be honest and say I'm infatuated with you. Please don't get up and walk out or think I'm a pervert. I'm not attached to anyone…not feeding you a line. Sometimes I'm too blunt. If you tell me to get lost, I will and hope you don't hate me or fire me."

"I'm flattered, Steve, but it's pretty early in the game for this. I don't know you and you don't know me. I find you attractive…no argument there, and I appreciate your honesty…but other than that, what do we know about each other?"

"I just killed all possible chances to get to know you better, haven't I? I know someone else loves you but I believe I could offer you much more than Mitch will ever be able to."

"What? Who?" Samantha set her drink down and covered her mouth to hide her desire to laugh.

"Mitch. Mitch Gillini. Didn't you know that?" Steve said innocently.

"Oh, Steve. Mitch and I have known each other since before we went to school. He lived two houses down from my family. I asked him to be my partner in my business because I've known him and know he is good at what he does in our field. We work well together. That's all there is to it."

"Lady, you need your eyes checked."

"Steve, I am in love with another man that you don't know. It isn't Mitch, Steve. I don't know what Mitch has told you but I think there is a total misunderstanding here," Samantha said, trying to straighten things out.

"Yeah, Mitch said it was a guy named Andy. Are you married to him? Has he proposed? Have you accepted? Are you…"

"Steve…please! What are you doing? I need to concentrate on this case. I thought that was why you suggested I join you tonight."

"Well, if the answer is no to my questions…why can't I at least try? I'm not trying to get you in bed. I like your personality as well and your looks. Yeah, Mitch told me what you had been through with the police department and how far you've come on your own. He said you are tough as nails on a case and in court, but a softy outside of work. You know there is more to life than work, and it appears you are missing out."

"Steve, we both have a job to do, and I expect you to do what I hired you to do. I think we need to end this conversation and evening. At least the part that includes me. I can catch a cab. Steve, I have enjoyed most of this time, but I need to go." Samantha started to stand when Steve took her hand.

"I'm sorry. Forget I've said any of this. I'll take you home."

The drive to Samantha's apartment went without words between them. She opened her car door to get out when

Steve stopped her. "I'm still a gentleman no matter what you think of me now. Stay here." He walked around to her side of the car, opened the door, and offered his hand to help her out. He walked her to the door.

"Steve, I don't want hard feelings between us. Let's just start all over as if this didn't happen. Mitch thinks you're the guy for this case, and I believe him. I didn't want someone from the Chicago force who might wonder what was going on and get nosy and ask questions."

"Mitch trusts your intuition and that's good enough for me. Let's just keep our relationship on a professional level. Thank you again for the evening."

Samantha turned to unlock the entrance door when Steve turned her around and kissed her gently. She pulled away and they looked at each other. Steve smiled and pulled her to him again and kissed her harder. Samantha didn't pull away.

16

“Good morning, Heather, is the boss in?” Mitch asked as he entered Samantha’s office.

“She’s on the phone, Mitch. Go on in.”

Samantha ended the phone conversation and motioned for Mitch to take a seat across from her desk. “Whatcha’ got?” She asked.

“All the info on Levi and Mueller and her sidekick.”

“Gosh…no bruises, broken bones, walking without crutches? Still have a job?”

“Smart ass! Yeah, I had no trouble getting what I needed. I was hoping the two secretaries would go on a coffee break so I could make copies, but that didn’t happen. Here’s the scoop.”

“Kanter was born here on the south side, no permanent address given for his early years, had various jobs throughout high school. Excelled in sports in college, enrolled in med school for post-grad work. He took night courses after he graduated from the police academy.”

“Somewhere along there, he took criminal justice courses and was hired by CPD. He went to day shift to work with kids in the Robert Taylor Homes project and Cabrini-Green. He organized basketball and baseball teams in the projects and other civic work after shift. Pretty much a stand-up guy."

"Levi…in medical school? Must have dropped out and now he's back on nights," Samantha reasoned.

"Three years in med school before dropping out. He wanted on the night shift. Had a couple of part-time jobs at hardware stores and other retail businesses. Almost a workaholic if you ask me."

"What about Mueller?"

"Born in Wisconsin, a couple of years in college, went to taxidermy school, lives at 117 Ellis Avenue. Interests include big game hunting and other mediocre stuff, been on the force eleven years. Made sergeant eight months ago. That's about it."

"And Officer Morton?"

"Morton graduated from high school, held a couple of jobs, graduated from the police academy. Pretty much in the background it seems. Worked nights for the last four years. Has an apartment on Harrison Street. All three of them have a spotless record."

"Seems like normal lives for the most part. But I see something that doesn't fit. You said Levi went to med school and Mueller studied taxidermy. Doesn't that seem a little odd? It does to me," Samantha said, pacing the office and going over what Mitch had told her. "Mitch, be a devil's advocate, why such severe career change for both of them?"

"Maybe Levi's parents wanted him to be a doctor or dentist. He tried it and didn't like it. Doesn't seem all that strange to me. And Mueller wanted to be a big game hunter but didn't like the idea of killing animals that are becoming extinct. Hell, I don't see anything off the wall with either one of them."

"Well, I do! Dr. Cullen told us that Kramer's skin had been meticulously removed as if a surgeon did it. With three years in med school, I'm sure he learned how to handle surgical instruments. And with Mueller's involvement with taxidermy, she would know a lot about removing just the skin and not a lot of tissue with it."

"Okay, I'm following your thinking. Where does Morton fit in?"

"I haven't figured that out yet. Maybe she isn't involved."

"I'm going to table this for a while and go visit Mrs. Kramer again. Just a one on one, woman to woman visit. Maybe she won't be so stiff and short with her answers."

"I'm off today and tomorrow. Holler if you need me." Mitch headed for the door.

Samantha pulled a pair of tan dress slacks from the hanger in her closet, a yellow turtleneck sweater from the chest of drawers and dark brown loafers from the shoe rack. Laying a light brown wool blazer on the bed to complete the outfit, she decided she looked casual enough to spend some one-on-one time with Mrs. Kramer.

"Mrs. Kramer, good morning," Samantha said with a smile. "Samantha O'Malley. May I come in?"

Mrs. Kramer remained still at the door for several seconds. Her stoic body and sharp facial features gave Samantha second thoughts about not calling ahead of her visit. Only Mrs. Kramer's eyes had softened at the sight of her.

"Yes, of course...come in." Her crisp German accent seemed promising to Samantha as she stepped into the foyer of the Kramer home. "I was just fixing my mid-morning cup of coffee. Would you like a cup?" Samantha thanked her and joined her at the kitchen table.

"And what news do you have for me about Otto's killer?"

"Nothing yet, Mrs. Kramer. That is why I'm here. I'd like you to tell me more about Otto's habits, his personal life as well as his work. I know he was devoted to his shop, and I imagine you were great support for him."

"Otto loved his work. He memorized his customer's likes and dislikes and their sizes, and offered suggestions as to colors that would accent their skin tones and hair color. He kept records of their past purchases to help guide them in buying new items."

"Mrs. Kramer, you speak with an accent. Where are you from?"

"I was born in Berlin, Germany. My family held positions in the German government."

"Is that where you met Otto?" Samantha asked as innocently as she could.

"Otto was a member of the...he had a business in my father's office. He was a businessman but knew my father and they often talked in his office."

"What did your father do?"

"He just held an office in government. Can I get you more coffee, Miss O'Malley?" She said looking away.

"No, this is plenty, thank you," Samantha answered. "Your home is so attractive and so beautifully decorated. Did you do the decorating or have a designer come?"

Samantha stood and investigated the other rooms hoping to get a tour.

"I did the decorating. Come, I will show you the rest of it."

Samantha followed Mrs. Kramer throughout the house and listened intently when she stopped to explain where she had purchased certain pieces of furniture.

"How long have you been in America?" Samantha asked as they walked.

"Somewhere around 1945."

"That must have been exciting going to Ellis Island and then to Chicago to start a new life and business." Samantha avoided eye contact as she baited Mrs. Kramer for information.

"We had friends already here before us. The Mil…" She stopped dead and realized what she was about to say. She quickly changed the subject.

"Please, let's go by the bedrooms. We have two bedrooms but rarely have overnight guests. Our bedroom is across from the guest room."

Samantha gazed at the draperies made from rich material. Then she noticed a pair of black high-top boots positioned partially under the bed by the nightstand. *Otto must have slept closest to the door*, she thought. The bedspread looked like the puffy lining of a casket and gawdy. Samantha noticed the pillow shams and that there was a small space between them.

She noticed the black end of something that resembled a gun. Mrs. Kramer caught Samantha looking in that direction and quickly led Samantha out of the room and down the hall back to the kitchen. Viewing the backyard from the kitchen window, she commented on the Kramer's back deck and the two beautiful weeping willow trees that Mitch had noticed the first time they interviewed Mrs. Kramer.

Looking down by the back door, Samantha caught another pair of black high-top shoes. It was as if Otto had just arrived home from his shop, took them off, and placed them by the door to the back entrance to be put on the next day.

"Detective O'Malley, did you hear me?" Mrs. Kramer asked.

"I'm sorry. What did you say?"

"Would you like another cup of coffee, or perhaps hot tea?"

"Oh, thank you, but no…I've taken enough of your time. I should be going. I really appreciate our time together and your hospitality. I hope you stay close to your friends here. You need to keep a social life. I believe Mr. Kramer would have wanted you to," Samantha said in a sympathetic voice. Mrs. Kramer opened the door for her and wished her a nice day.

As soon as Samantha's car was out of sight, she pulled over along the curb and radioed Mitch to meet her at her office as soon as possible.

"What's up, boss?" Mitch said as he entered Samantha's office. "You sounded like it was important."

"I just left Mrs. Kramer's house. I took a chance to make a social visit in hopes I could see another side of her."

"Well, did you?" Mitch asked.

"Yes, and two pair of black high-top military-style boots were in a bedroom upstairs and by the back door! The kind the Nazis wore during the war. The kind Otto was wearing when he was killed. The same ones that have disappeared from the evidence room and log. Dr. Cullen told me himself that he saw the boots, and Jami in the evidence room remembers logging them in."

"I think Otto Kramer was more than a random murder. I think he was a high-ranking Nazi! I've got to find those boots and check the heels to see if there is a cavity that could hold a cyanide pill in it."

"And you still think Levi Kanter is involved?"

"Up to his eyeballs. It is all making sense," Samantha said, standing by the open Kramer file on her desk. "Mitch, look at these photos of the crime scene. Look at this one that shows Michigan Ave. This is Levi's squad car and that's him looking back at us when we first responded. Why is he even there? Morton and Mueller's shifts had ended and Levi should have been off shift too."

"Why was he there and still using a department squad car? And something else. His lieutenant obviously…" Just then, Heather came into Samantha's office and said Steve Jordon was on line one.

"Yes, Steve," Samantha said, putting the phone on speaker.

"I think you better get here. Officer Kanter is inside the warehouse. I don't think he is alone."

Samantha backed out of her parking space and took the back streets to Clark Street. She drove into the alley that led to the warehouse and parked behind Steve Jordon's car. Mitch stayed on Clark Street and parked along the front of the warehouse. Getting out of his car, he saw Levi's vehicle parked on the other side of the street.

He met up with Samantha, and the two of them walked to the warehouse dock. Samantha drew her weapon, opened the door, and listened.

She heard nothing, so she walked in with her weapon drawn. Mitch, with his weapon drawn, followed. They saw Steve at the far end of the warehouse by the door that led to the partitioned rooms. She motioned for him to step aside as she approached and peered through the primitive hole that was eye-level to her.

Three people were working in one of the rooms designed like the holding rooms for Jews to shower in at the Auschwitz death camp. The door was partially closed so she could only see two figures but heard three distinctively different voices. She knew Levi was the one looking at the piping above the two benches in the room.

She couldn't make out all of what he was saying. The second person was wearing an oversized heavy jacket, was tall, and had broad shoulders, but she couldn't see his face. She stepped back and motioned for Jordon to look. After a few minutes, Jordon walked over to her.

"Levi is giving the tall man directions on drilling holes in the support pillar that was in each of the three rooms," Jordon whispered and went on. "The tall man is the one I saw driving the van the night Levi and he went into the warehouse for twenty minutes or so. I can't see his face but I know it's him by his walk. I hear someone else asking questions but can't see him."

Mitch walked up to the two of them and whispered, "What's going on in there?"

"Three men are in there discussing the shower setup. One is Levi. We don't know who the other two are. But one of their voices sounds familiar to me," Samantha whispered. "Damn, they are turning and coming toward the door. We gotta get out of here!"

"We could stop them and ask what they are doing. Trespassing for one thing," Mitch said.

"No, we don't have enough on them, yet. It's their word against ours. We know there are three involved. That's a good start. We can connect the warehouse with Levi, giving us probable cause for a search warrant for the warehouse. All we need to find is evidence on Levi."

They went back to their cars and backed out of the alley before Levi and the other two men left the building. Mitch parked by the fountain on Seymore Street, and the three met at Mitch's car to discuss their next move.

"Ok, we need as much as we can on Levi. It's too late to check the dumpster behind his building. If he threw away anything, it's long gone and in the landfill. The boots are in Mrs. Kramer's house. We'll get a search warrant for her house. I'm sure the two pairs of boots are Otto's."

"The gun I saw may be his, too. We may be approaching third base but we can't head for home plate until we have enough on Levi to make an arrest."

Mitch and Samantha drove to her office in silence. Mitch felt she was thinking about how to get solid evidence on Levi and chose not to interrupt her thoughts.

But the look on her face said there was something more on her mind. Something more personal. When they reached the office, Mitch turned off the engine but didn't get out.

"Sam, you were pretty short with Steve back at the warehouse. Earlier you didn't want to talk to him. Is something going on there that I can't see but sure as heck can sense?"

After several moments of staring out her car window, Samantha broke her silence.

"I'm afraid."

"You afraid? Ha! I've seen you in action. You aren't afraid of anything!"

"Yes, I am, Mitch. I'm afraid of life. I was told, recently, that I am not living life. I'm afraid of failure in my job. I'm afraid of ridicule. I'm afraid of not being wanted. I'm afraid of letting go of my emotions, my desires. I don't want to hurt anyone that is close to me or that I really care about. When I look at myself in the mirror, I can see that it's true. All of it is true, and I don't know what to do about it."

A small tear trickled down her cheek when he looked at her. "I've never heard you, ever, express what you considered your shortcomings out loud. You are always the one to uplift someone else up; always the one to encourage those who felt they couldn't continue in reaching their goals; never chastising yourself. Would you like to go someplace quiet and have a drink? I'm here to listen and help wherever I can."

"No, I need to get back to work. I need to be prepared for tonight."

"Okay, but what has all of this got to do with Steve Jordon?"

"Steve was the one who said I wasn't living life when we went out to dinner the other night."

17

“Let me get this straight…out of the blue, Steve said you aren’t living life?”

“Not exactly. We were just talking and he started asking what I thought to be personal questions. It bothered me. So, I told him I was going to catch a cab. He didn’t need to leave and take me home. At his insistence, he did anyway and apologized. I thanked him for dinner but said we needed to keep our relationship professional. He knew about Andy.”

“When I unlocked the building entrance and said goodnight, he took my arm, turned me around, and kissed me. Mitch, I pushed him away, but he pulled me to him again and kissed me harder. I didn’t push back that time. I liked the kiss. I wanted more…a lot more! Knowing this, I felt like a cheat.”

“This would kill Andy. I haven’t told him. I’m afraid to.” Samantha’s voice cracked as she bit her trembling lip between words.

“Sam, you aren’t a bad person. It was all right to feel good about the kiss. You are human, a woman with feelings, with a body and mind that has feelings, emotions, reactions. There is nothing wrong with you.”

“What do I do now, Mitch? I’m so confused.”

"That's up to you. I can't answer that. Give it time and see what happens. You can't avoid Jordon, he's part of this case now. It will be over in a few weeks…I firmly believe that. We are so close to solving it. Steve Jordon will be back in Joliet and not with us. As far as Andy goes, I'm not saying a thing to him. That's all up to you."

"You said he would be traveling out of the country again in a week or so. When he's gone, that will give you time to sort things out with your thoughts and emotions. Please stop beating yourself up over this. Something I see is that maybe now you are living life. Maybe you are letting the woman in you take charge instead of the professional need to solve a horrible homicide and prove your worth in doing so."

"You don't owe this city, the police department, me or anyone else anything."

Mitch saw the tears coming through her squinted eyes and pulled her to him and let her cry.

"Sam, I confess I love you too. I've loved you since we were kids. My parents called it puppy love, but it never went away. I used to think I'd like to be in Andy's shoes sometimes, but my affection, now, is different. I would never try to take you from Andy. Maybe because we think alike most of the time."

"We are both very good in our work and we work great together. My affection is more protection and respect for you. Not just because you're a woman but as my partner. I look at that as love too."

"In Steve's case, he's infatuated with you and yet respects you very much. Maybe the night and the mood just caught up with him. Don't fault him for the feelings he and other guys have toward you. They are human too."

Samantha dried her eyes and reached for the car door. "I'll try to put all of this in perspective tomorrow. Wasn't there a line something like that in some movie…'I'll worry about that tomorrow'."

Mitch, grinning, nodded his head. "Yeah, *Gone with the Wind*, I believe. That was a famous line said by Scarlett O'Hara."

"Well, that's what I will do! I'll worry about that tomorrow! Tonight, it is business. We are about to blast this case wide open, and if my instincts are right, we will know the killer. I just pray we learn why Otto Kramer was murdered."

Samantha stopped to fill Heather in and the plans for the night then went to her apartment.

"Hey, Arthur, I'm home. Let's have lunch on the balcony. You get the salmon deluxe dinner for cats, and I get the PBJ sandwich. You're getting the better deal, believe me." Just then, the phone rang.

18

"Miss O'Malley?"

"Yes. Who's calling?"

"This is Officer Morton. Remember me? I was with Sgt. Mueller the night your apartment was broken into."

"What do you want?"

"Are you still on the Otto Kramer case?"

"Yes."

"I have something to tell you."

"Start talking. I'm listening."

"Not on the phone. There is a little café on Seymore Street across from Wrigley Field. The game should be over in thirty minutes or so. Can you meet me there?"

"Yes. Make sure you are alone, Morton. If I see anyone else with you, you won't see me."

"Yes, Ma'am. I'll be alone."

Samantha pressed the connection button and dialed Mitch's number. "I just talked to Officer Morton. She has something to tell me about the Kramer case. We are going to meet at the café on Clark Street. She's supposed to be alone. You live closer to it than I do. Can you go and watch for her and spot anyone else that might be with her or already inside?"

"I know the owners. I'll be there and have it set up. What time will she be there?"

"Thirty minutes."

"Shit! Not much time. I'll send our code over your radio if I sense a setup. Be careful."

Fifteen minutes later, Mitch radioed his position that all looked good. He had seen Morton enter the cafe by herself. The owner was to seat her in the back. Samantha parked her car a couple of blocks away and took the alley to the café. She entered through the back door and sat across from Officer Morton in a booth.

"Okay, what have you got, Morton?"

"I know you don't like me, Miss O'Malley. Even so, please hear me out on this. I have to talk to someone. I thought it was a game, but it got out of hand. I didn't realize what I was getting into. I…"

"Get on with it, Morton. This isn't a pity party and I'm not a priest."

"Well, a year ago, Officer Kanter told us some stories about the death camps in Germany. He went into a lot of detail telling of the horrible things that were done to Jews and people with physical and mental issues. One of the most horrific things was removing the skin from the Jewish men's torsos and backs. I thought it was odd that Levi would joke about it. He went on to say that he thought we…"

"Who is we, Morton?"

"Well, it was Sgt. Mueller, me, and Officer Levi Kanter. Officer Kanter thought we should find a German guy and scare him into thinking we were going to skin him! It was supposed to be just a game, Miss O'Malley. Not something that he would do for real!"

"Last winter, when we were on patrol, he radioed the sergeant to have her meet him in the alley by Otto Kramer's store. I was riding with Sgt. Mueller, so I heard the whole conversation. The sergeant agreed to meet him. We were in the alley at closing time, but Kramer never came out. We waited until we received another call and left. It got busy, and we never returned."

"About a week later, we tried again, all the time Levi and the sergeant laughed about doing this. A few days later, the sergeant told me to call in sick, that she, Kanter, and I were going to scare Kramer. We parked behind the store and waited until he came out. I remember it was well after midnight before Mr. Kramer came out."

"When he came around the corner to walk to his car, which was parked at the end of the alley, Kanter grabbed him and covered his mouth with a rag soaked in chloroform. Mr. Kramer tried to holler and get free, but by then Sgt. Mueller was holding him too…then he passed out. They laid him down and took his boots off."

"Levi took his flashlight and studied the heel of the shoe. I never did know why he did that. God, I want to forget I ever saw what happened next."

"Keep going, Morton."

"I swear to you, this was supposed to be a game. They weren't supposed to skin him!"

"Why Kramer? What was the significance of Kramer being skinned?"

"Well, Levi went crazy and told Sgt. Mueller to work faster."

"What do you mean, work faster?"

"The sergeant knew how to skin animals. She was a hunter before she was a cop. Levi wanted her to take the skin off Mr. Kramer. I was getting sick and wanted to leave but the sergeant wouldn't let me. She reminded me that the chief has no use for lesbians, and we would be fired if he knew about us."

"You mean Sgt. Mueller and you are lesbian partners…right?"

"Yes, but we live separately so no one knows."

"Ok, now why did Levi single out Otto Kramer?"

"Henrich Miller was the first one several months ago. Sgt. Mueller just told me about it. I wasn't there. Levi, as I said, went crazy and had this hideous laugh. He kept calling Mr. Kramer a Nazi bastard. Over and over. Then he said, 'I got Miller, I'll get you. You can't hurt anyone else ever again'."

"Okay, Morton. You know you will be held as an accomplice in this. I can't prevent that, but I can see about you having a lighter sentence because you came to me with this. Morton, is Levi planning any more attacks like this?"

"Yes, he told us there is one more that he wants to get when the time is right."

"So, Levi is after Nazis that have escaped capture from the war? Did you know this all along?"

"Not at first. I didn't until he killed Mr. Kramer. Sgt. Mueller told me when we took the skins to Kahn's tailor shop."

"What do you mean? What does Mr. Kahn have to do with this?"

"He takes the skins and makes them into lampshades."

"What?"

"Yes, Miss O'Malley. He was an Auschwitz death camp survivor like Levi and…"

"Wait, wait, wait. Levi was in Auschwitz?"

"Yes. The stories he told us were from there. Both Levi and Mr. Kahn saw horrible things done to Jews like them."

"Okay, go on about Mr. Kahn."

"Mr. Kahn dries the skins, then dyes them different colors. When done, he sells them back to the German people. He said he is getting even for what they did. The Germans that buy them don't know what they are. I'm so sorry to have been a part of this." Officer Morton began to cry.

"Oh my god!" Samantha gave Morton a Kleenex and let her cry. "You said there is one more. Do you mean Levi is planning this soon?"

"I don't know when or who. He tells the sergeant his plans, not me. I just heard him say 'One more to go and I will be done'."

"Is there anything else, Morton?"

"One more thing. Levi is the reason there was a chemical spill in that warehouse. He knocked over a big tank when he was moving plywood in. He didn't know what was in the tank, but the regulator was knocked off when the tank hit the floor and a fluid came out that had been pressurized. He got scared and called it in."

"What was he doing in there?"

"Oh, God, I wish I was dead." Morton buried her head in her hands.

"Take it easy, Morton. Just tell me what he was doing."

"He was making a...gas chamber in the warehouse. The plywood was to make individual rooms like the ones in Auschwitz. He and two others ran lines to pump deadly gas into the rooms. They looked like shower rooms with benches. He said they were modeled after the ones he saw in Auschwitz. Levi said he was ten years old, but he witnessed horrible things that the Nazis did to men, women, and even kids that he could never forget."

"Have you seen the other two who are involved in this?"

"No. He just told Sgt. Mueller about them as they were being built."

"So, you have no idea who was helping him?"

"No. No names were ever mentioned. I'm in a lot of trouble, aren't I?"

"Will you keep me informed as to when the next one is to happen and where?"

"Yes, Ma'am. I'm telling you the truth. I was forced to watch. Levi said he would tell Chief Van Watson about the sergeant and me if I told. I never touched Mr. Kramer. I would only watch and then drive the sergeant to Mr. Kahn's shop with the skins. This was supposed to be a game. That's all, I swear."

"I know this has been hard on you to tell me. I will say nothing to anyone at this point. You can go now. And thank you." Samantha started to leave, stopped, and went back to Morton.

"Officer Morton, it was you and Mueller who broke into my apartment, wasn't It?"

"Yes. Levi made us do it."

"Where was Levi?"

"He was in a dry-cleaning van with someone else, but I don't know who that was."

"What was he looking for?"

"He was wanting whatever you had on Mr. Kramer and Mr. Miller. He was worried that you suspected he was involved somehow."

"Thanks, Morton." Samantha left the café through the back.

She met Mitch in the alley and briefed him on what Morton had told her.

"My God! Levi is the killer! Just like you suspected. I never would have thought that. He just doesn't seem the type with all his civic work."

"Can't judge a book by its cover, Mitch. When I went to see Mrs. Kramer the other day, she mentioned that she was having a lampshade made to match the other fabrics in the room. She must be getting it from Kahn's tailor shop! Can you imagine what she's going to think when she finds out the shade is made from...her husband's skin!"

"Evil breeds evil," Samantha added.

19

"There's her ride to the concert. It's 2040. As soon as she is out of sight, I'll go."

"Sam, if you go in there illegally, it will never hold up in court. The defense will tear you apart. They'll ruin your reputation and you'll probably lose your license. Think what the chief would say if he found out."

"I must know if those are the boots Otto was wearing. There were salt stains on the ones he had on. If either pair has that on then, then they are his boots. If there is a cavity in the heel for a cyanide pill, then all the better. Yeah, it's illegal but I'll use the fact that I saw the boots when I had the house tour. That alone is probable cause."

"Send our code to my radio if someone is coming toward the house. I know where the boots are, so it won't take but two or three minutes and I'm out."

Mitch waited in the alley by the Kramer garage and watched Samantha enter the back door. It didn't look like she had to break in. He saw the glow from her flashlight in the window of the back porch. Samantha picked up the boots by the door and looked at the heels. Her flashlight showed the hollowed-out section that would have hidden a cyanide pill.

She took a hairpin and pried the cover open. The cavity on both boots was empty. She replaced them by the door like she found them. Quietly, she walked to the bedroom where she had seen a pair of high-top boots partly under the bed. She pulled them out and checked the heels. They too had a center compartment like the first pair.

Again, she pried both compartments open to see if there were cyanide pills in them. Only the right boot held a pill. The toes had remnants of salt from the sidewalk and alley. She placed them back under the bed. Quickly, she left the house, left the door as she found it, and joined Mitch in his car.

"That went well, and the back door was unlocked. Maybe she always leaves it that way. So, I didn't break in. I just hope there is more evidence at Levi's apartment. It's almost 2100 hours. You said Levi was scheduled to work, so we have time to check his place."

"Division Street is not part of his patrol district, but I don't trust him or the other two. One or all of them could show up at his apartment for some reason. He wouldn't dare call in to say where he was. If we could just find something that has his DNA on it."

"I have Steve Jordon watching the apartment. He's off today. Let's get something to eat. Lunch was a long time ago. How hungry are you?"

"I'm too pumped up to eat but coffee sounds good. Let's go to the Diner."

"Headed that way. What judge are you looking at for the search warrants? Judge Geister always supports the police, and he knows…whoa!" Mitch slowed to a stop and backed up.

"Well, would you look at that. Officer Kanter has parked his car in a tow-away space! Hot damn!" Mitch reached for the car radio and requested a tow truck to his location.

"Damn. It will be an hour before they can get here." He drove up to the corner, put his caution lights on, and walked to the phone booth.

"Hello, Pete? Mitch Gillini, Pete. Do you have a tow truck available?"

"Sure, Mitch. Whatcha got?"

"Meet me at the corner of Clark and State streets. There is a beige Ford car parked in a tow-away zone. I need it towed to your garage ASAP! When you get it inside, lower your garage door. I and Detective O'Malley will meet you there."

"Why are you wanting it brought here? Shouldn't I take it to the police compound?"

"No, I don't want it at the police compound…this is a special car."

"Okay…see you at the garage."

While they waited, Mitch called the dispatcher and had her run the plates.

"Detective Gillini, the car is registered to a Levy Cantor on Division Street."

"Spell the first and last name, please."

"L-e-v-y C-a-n-t-o-r."

"Thank you."

"Sam, listen to this. Levi's actual name is Levy Cantor. He's Jewish, Sam! Officer Morton said he was a Holocaust survivor, right?"

"Yep. Kramer was a German Nazi, and I'll bet he was the guard at Auschwitz. Levi knew him from there and saw him commit despicable crimes. He has spent all these years hunting Kramer down. Now he's got Mueller helping him, and Morton too."

Mitch and Samantha waited for the tow truck to arrive and followed it to Pete's shop.

"What's so special about this car? Sure, doesn't have much re-sell value," Pete questioned when the car was inside.

"I want to open the glove compartment and the trunk. Illinois law requires it towed to do that legally," Samantha explained.

Samantha opened the glove compartment and pulled out the stuff that was crammed in it. "He doesn't take care of the car. Hasn't had the oil changed in seven thousand miles. Look at the gauge. Oh, look what I found! A small bottle of chloroform, disposable gloves, and two rags that have a faint smell of chloroform."

"Pete, can you pull out the front seats? Maybe there is something under them." Samantha placed the chloroform, gloves, and rags in a bag and put it on the hood of the car.

A few minutes later, Pete stepped away from the car. "There's nothing under the front seats, Miss O'Malley."

"Okay. Pete, use a wrecking bar on the trunk. I want this baby opened!"

"Whatcha lookin' for?"

"Evidence in a homicide, Pete. Keep quiet about it, you hear?"

"I know nothing, Miss O'Malley. That's why I'm still above ground."

After a few tries to pop the trunk, it opened. Mitch started searching through the contents. "Here's a long wool coat. Double breasted with what looks like brass buttons. It's been here a long time. Hey, here's a briefcase. One of the clasps is gone."

Mitch laid the coat on a work bench and pulled the briefcase out. "Remember the clasp that we found in the alley when we were searching for clues? You did keep it, didn't you?"

"Yeah, but Cindy didn't find a fingerprint on it. It's in the evidence box in the evidence room. Can you get the other one to open?"

"Working on it now. It's packed with documents. Look at this. Documents showing Kramer had his name changed from Kratz. Here's his entry papers to America. Mrs. Kramer's is attached. Looks like Kramer was a high-ranking officer for the Nazis. Here, read this stuff. Some of it is in German."

"These documents have a Wolfgang Mitzler named as a Doctor of Medicine. I wonder if that could be Himmey Miller? Mrs. Kramer almost let that name slip when visited the other day. Here's a list of numbers and items. Looks like watches, maybe rings and wallets."

"The numbers may be those that were tattooed on the Jews and the items taken from them. Mitch, we have to get a subpoena for Levi's residence. We have more than enough proof for a search. It's 2202. I'm calling Judge Geist tonight. Pete, hold the car. It doesn't go anywhere. Nobody touches it, got it! Even if you must sleep in the chair, over there, all night."

"If there is a problem, you call me. I don't care what time it is."

The judge agreed that there was cause for an all-inclusive search warrant for Levi's residence and car. He issued another warrant for the Kramer residence to expire in fifty-six hours of issuance, giving the detectives plenty of time for a thorough search of both places.

20

Across town, early morning.

"I have Danish breads when you are ready to eat. Coffee is already in your cup. I must tell you, I watched your facial expressions change over the several months you've been coming, and I'm pleased to see you are looking so good. Even a smile on your face. The medication must be doing you some good. Oh, what is this? For me?"

"I brought you a plant. You don't have one like this. It won't bear fruit or bloom but will live a long time. The florist said so. I hope you like it."

"I do, I do. It will look very nice on the bookcase over here. It will have plenty of sun, too."

"Yes, the medication you gave me has helped. I want to thank you for doing so. Today is my birthday."

"Well, my goodness! Happy birthday! Are you going to be with friends today and do something special?"

"Probably not. I have one more task to do. I will complete my work in a couple of days, I think. To be done will be a great present from me to myself."

"Tell me about your birthdays when you were in the camp. What did the soldiers do for you?"

"Nothing. They didn't know about it. No one celebrated their birthdays. Nothing but work, hunger, and death there. But I did reminisce about my fifth birthday. It's the first one that I remember. My mother always made special cakes. Some of our friends went to work early in the morning, so she would make Latke cakes with juice."

"They would stop in on their way to work and eat breakfast with us. Most came in the evening after work. Mom made noodle kugel with onion soup. It's a very filling dish. There were cookies and tea afterward. I would receive a present of two and their kids and I would play for a while."

"On my tenth birthday in the camp, I was moved to another building. I was growing and getting tall like my father, and I was strong for my age. I moved in with boys ages ten and up. There were twenty-one with me there. It was crowded sometimes. We each had our own bunk only when one or two of the boys didn't return after their hours were up in the hospital."

"The older boys said they were probably killed for getting upset at what they saw. Our building was close to the hospital, and our work was to assist the doctors. It should have been called the butcher shop for what happened there."

"What was your job in the hospital? Seems an odd place for young boys to work."

"The doctors in the hospital performed experiments on the Jewish people, the mentally ill, and other people the Nazis saw as unfit to live. Our job was to carry a bucket and pick up body parts and organs that weren't of use in the experiments. When our bucket was full, we took it to the burn pit."

"We were to keep our heads down, not look at what was going on, and not speak to one another or tell anyone what was being done to the patients there. If we did talk, it was certain death for us. But we did see what was going on. Patients having surgical experiments done on them with no pain medication. The screams, the begging to kill them went on the entire day or night we worked."

"I saw one doctor, Dr. Mengele, take notes as his victims suffered from injecting chemicals in them. An example would be injecting shots of chemicals in children's eyes to change the color. After a few hours, maybe a day, he would check the results. It never worked. He'd get mad and kill the child."

"Then I or another boy would come with our bucket and take the body to the burn pit. He would write about the experiment and the results in a notebook. He had a bookshelf in his office that held all the notebooks. Again, the smell of burning flesh filled our building."

"It was so close to the burn pit. Smoke wrapped the camp in a gray cloud that the sun couldn't penetrate. I have wondered if anyone ever found those notebooks."

"Other doctors specialized in castrating teenage boys with no pain medication. Their reactions seemed to excite the doctors. The boys were like sick animals afterward. If they died from the shock, they were dissected, and the doctors would take notes for future studies. Those that survived were studied for a few days then taken out of the hospital and shot."

"There were always new victims to keep experiments going on. These notes were proof that the Jews, in particular, had undesirable genetics and were useless to be kept. The overall consensus was the Jewish race tainted the Aryan race."

"Sometimes I worked in the women's section. Lobotomies were performed daily on teenage girls. Their sex organs were removed, and if they survived, they were nothing but zombies roaming the halls of the hospital. That doctor, Mengele, liked pregnant women. Those that were about to give birth were under his care."

"He would deliver the baby, and if it was a single birth, he would kill it immediately. He wanted twins and would scream at everyone when there were no twins born that day. He liked to keep the twins under observation. One baby would be fed normally and the other no food was given. He wanted to see how long it took for it to die from starvation. I hated working there. I hated him."

"This is very hard on you. The memories that haunt you have taken their toll. I'm so sorry you have lived through this. Looking over my past sessions with you, I see where you have mentioned your mother only twice. Did you see her or were you able to contact her?"

"My mother was in the women's section. She had gone mad by now. In almost three years at Auschwitz, she had two babies. One of those babies would have been my brother or sister."

"You see, she was pregnant when we were removed from our village. I remember her crying and holding her stomach the day we left. I thought she was sick, but in fact, she was pregnant. The second pregnancy was a result of the continual rapes by the Nazis."

"I switched shifts with another boy when I found out where she was. It was night-time and dark in the area she was in. I walked through the tables until I found her on a gurney. I whispered to her that I was there. She turned her head toward me but her eyes didn't really see me. They were lost to some other world."

"I held her hand and told her I loved her and moved on down the row of tables and gurneys. I stayed behind when I saw her wheeled into the delivery room, and I continued to pick up things on the floor to appear busy. The doctor cut her open and took the baby. It was a single birth and of no value. It was put in a sink and soon died."

"From the corner of the room where I stood unnoticed, I saw the assistant to the doctor put a bag over her head and tie it under her chin. I saw who it was. There was a name on his white coat. I heard the doctor say, 'She is of no use to us anymore.' I covered my mouth to keep from yelling at him. It was all I could do to keep from crying."

"I knew if I cried out, he would kill me. I never saw where they took her. She had lived in hell her entire time in the camp. Surely heaven's gates were opened for her."

"So, you see the memories, the sounds, the smells are still fresh. But more vivid are the faces of the evil so-called humans who committed these crimes. What bothers me most are those that escaped capture after the war. They are out there living a good life, no nightmares, sleeping peacefully at night, having families, and hiding their true identity. Feeling no regrets for their crimes."

"I was still in prison after the war but had found a way out. I know where the guard and one of the doctors who tortured me, my parents, and all the others who couldn't defend themselves are. I am doing what wasn't done to them after the war. I want them to feel the pain those incapable of helping themselves felt!"

"Earlier today, I said I saw a change in you. Your facial expressions had changed from when you first started coming to therapy. Now I'm concerned. You have that look you used to have. There is fire in your eyes."

"Yes, I am full of fire. I know these criminals. I have seen them and watched them. I know how they move, how they walk, how they laugh."

"You have seen them here in Chicago?"

"Yes! Listen to me. They have businesses here. They are earning a living here. They think they got away from punishment for their acts of evil. Oh no! I won't permit that. They are going to suffer! I have taken care of two of them and now only one more to go. One more and I can sleep at night. I won't have dreams, I won't smell burning flesh, rotting flesh, or blood."

"Have devoted my life to this, and I have achieved my goals. When I am done, I will have rid the world of three more evil men."

"This is wrong! Your way is wrong! They are war criminals and will be treated in the proper manner according to the law. Not the way you have chosen."

"It is the right way, the only way! Don't try to stop me. One more, that's all! You know nothing in your enclosed castle with the warmth of family, your walnut desk, your leather chair, the plush carpet you sink your Italian-made shoes in. You know nothing!"

"Please, please, let me take you to the right people. They can do this for you and take care of you, too."

"Why should I care what happens to me? I have no life. Whatever you do won't be enough. Time is running out; I must finish the job! I must go now."

He stood and slowly walked to the door as if in a trance. Never saying goodbye or waving. He walked through the door and silently closed it as a parent would to not wake a sleeping child.

21

The phone rang in Samantha's office.

"O'Malley Investigations, Heather speaking, may I help you?"

"I need to speak to Miss O'Malley. It's urgent!"

"I'll transfer. Samantha, line 1."

"Hello?"

"Miss O'Malley? This is Officer Morton. I know there is going to be another murder. I don't know who it is but I know Levi Kanter is going to do it. I was at Sgt. Mueller's apartment when Levi and the sergeant were planning it. It's going to be tonight. Somewhere on Clark Street."

"Levi said a warehouse. I don't know if that is the place for sure but that's what they said. All three of us work tonight. I'm really scared!"

"Okay, Morton. If you can confirm the location, let me know. Be careful! Oh, if anyone else is involved, let me know."

Samantha replaced the phone receiver and went into Heather's office. The office door opened and Mitch walked in carrying a box of donuts.

"Hope you two are hungry. Hate to have to eat six of these."

"Mitch, forget the donuts and have a seat in my office. Heather, is there any coffee left?"

"I'll make a fresh pot and bring it to you."

Mitch followed Samantha into her office. Samantha closed her office door and pulled out a city map and circled a city block around Clark Street.

"Morton called a few minutes ago and said there is going to be another murder tonight. Levi and Mueller were planning it. Morton didn't know who was to be killed but for sure tonight."

"She stated the Levi mentioned the warehouse. All three of them are on duty tonight. Get a hold of Jordon. Make sure he is available when he's off shift."

"How are we going to set up for this if we don't know the location for sure?"

"Morton is to call me back when she knows for sure. I have a blown-up picture of the city block that includes the warehouse on Clark Street. There are just a few businesses along the side of the street the warehouse is on. Levi constructed those chamber rooms inside the warehouse. That's got to be the place! Across the street is a rental shop and a gas station."

"That's about it. A few empty lots on either side of the warehouse and tall weeds around them. Oh, the city is using the lot directly south of the warehouse dock for maintenance trucks and equipment. No one will be around there working. If the warehouse is the place, then the empty lot would be a good place for one of you guys to be at."

"So, we can't do anything until Morton confirms the place. I don't understand why Levi didn't say where when the three of them were together," Mitch asked as he stood looking up from the map. "I'm not sure I believe Morton."

"I believe her. My guess is Levi doesn't trust Morton. She doesn't handle situations well. And she doesn't like the position she's in with these killings. She and Mueller knew who the other two would be, but for some reason, Levi is remaining mum on this one, and so far, where they plan to do this. She said twice that Levi avoided giving the name of the person, even to Mueller."

Samantha buzzed Heather to come in.

"Heather, can Mitch use your car overnight? You can have mine if you need it."

"Sure, Mitch, as long as you wash it before you return it." Heather smiled and sat two cups of coffee down.

"Good. None of them know your car, Heather, so anyone showing up and seeing it for some reason, will ignore it." The office phone rings.

"Samantha, line 1 again," Heather said.

"O'Malley."

"It's the warehouse tonight, Miss O'Malley! I'm positive. Sgt. Mueller told me when she dropped me off at my apartment," Morton said in a shaken voice. "Miss O'Malley, you can stop the killing, can't you?"

"Okay, Morton. Relax. Is there anything else she said? Did she mention the victim's name?"

"No, honest. Just that we had to go to the warehouse after shift briefing."

"Okay, Morton, just be yourself and don't let on you have talked to me." Samantha hung the phone up and looked at Mitch.

"Well, that's what we were waiting for…it's the warehouse."

"Sam, have you given any thought to this being a setup to get you?" Mitch asked. "You are putting a lot of faith in Morton's phone calls. What if the chief has them working against you?"

"First of all, she hates her involvement in this. She wants out and is being blackmailed into participating. Second, I can't believe Levi would have built the chambers to get me there in a secluded building, even if he thinks I'm on to him. What would the point be? He could have had killed me months ago before anyone put two and two together. Yes, I believe her."

"Mitch, the three of us should meet behind the rental shop at 2300 hours. It's directly across the street from the warehouse. It will be very dark then. We'll have time to go over everything and get in our positions."

"We are assuming he will do this during his shift. Right?" Mitch asked.

"I would assume during his shift. It would be 0700 hours when he's off, and daylight. He can cover himself better with a sound alibi during his shift. The same for Mueller and Morton. They could lie on their shift reports for the time they are with Levi. It all makes sense."

"The construction of the chambers within the warehouse. The other two murders were by the victims' businesses. He has changed the MO and maybe drawing the person to a secluded place instead. And the work Levi has done inside. And he and Mueller were talking the warehouse," Samantha thought out loud.

"Yeah, and there have been heavy patrols on Michigan Avenue since the other two murders. Or, maybe to throw us off if he thinks you are suspecting him or the three of them. I remember you became suspicious of all three after your apartment was broken into. Okay, but I still think this could be a set up. See you at 2300." Mitch left the office to swap cars with Heather.

At 2200 hours, Samantha was ready. Bulletproof vest on and her Colt Python .357 at her side.

She went through several possible scenarios in her mind as to how the confrontation could go down. She felt secure that she had covered all bases. Her only wish was to know who the victim was going to be ahead of time. She went downstairs and knocked on Mrs. Henricks' apartment door.

"Yes, can I help…oh, Samantha, good evening."

"Mrs. Hendricks, I'm going to be gone for several hours tonight, working. I may not return until sometime in the morning. I'll do my best to not disturb you when I do get back. Mitch may be with me as well."

"That's fine. Tomorrow is Friday, and I'll be up early making the cinnamon rolls as usual for all of you. Samantha, are you alright? You aren't smiling…such a serious look on your face."

Samantha smiled. "I think we will wrap up this case tonight. At least I hope so. Don't worry, I'll be okay," Samantha said as she kissed Mrs. Henricks forehead. "Get some sleep." She was about to leave the apartment when she heard the phone rang. She ran back upstairs thinking it was Mitch or Steve.

"Hey, babe, how about a late dinner tonight? I'm two hours from Chicago and with traffic, I won't get back into Chicago until midnight at the earliest tonight."

"Andy, I won't be here. I'm hopefully wrapping this case up tonight. You have your key with you as I have no idea when I'll get back. I'm leaving a couple of lights on."

"Wow, another possible murder like the other two?"

"I don't know for sure. Just going on an informant's information."

"You sound so businesslike…you okay?"

"Yeah. Is that all?"

"Well, I guess so. Did I interrupt something?" Andy asked, puzzled at Samantha's tone.

"No, I just have a lot on my mind. Can we talk later?"

"Sure. Bye." Andy hung up the phone, trying to digest the conversation. Samantha never sounded like that before. He knew the case was coming to a head and with the tone Samantha had, he sensed it wouldn't end well for someone. A cold chill ran through him when he thought Samantha could be hurt or maybe worse. She didn't say I love you or even goodbye.

He reached her apartment shortly after midnight. No word or call on how things were going, and he knew better than to call her. It wasn't the first time she had been short with him when she was working on a case. He should be used to this by now but he wasn't. It just wasn't like her. He got out of his car and leaned against it.

It was a warm, clear night and the gentle breeze felt good. He tried to think of his life without her, and cases like this one made him wonder if he could live with the demands of her career. Would she slow down if they married?

He felt sure she wouldn't, and deep inside he only wanted for her what she wanted. What made her happy and fulfilled. He would marry her in a minute then wondered if that would ever happen. She had put him off so many times before he stopped asking. She had learned to live with his career, spending so many weeks, maybe months, out of the country. They both had demanding jobs.

He had to get over the fear. He had waited three years; he knew he would continue to do so.

He watched as cars drove by thinking that the next one would be Samantha but they didn't pull in her drive. His heart leaped each time one slowed down. He got back in his car, rolled the window down so he would hear her when she did arrive, and tried to think of other things. Surely, she wouldn't be much longer.

22

"You both ready? It's 2330 hours. Shift briefing should be over. The three of them should be in their squad cars. Our cars will be fine behind the rental shop. It's very dark in their back parking lot. I'll be inside behind the cylinders so I can see the victim when he or she comes in," Samantha said as she picked up her car keys and opened the apartment door.

"See you later, Samantha. Be careful," Steve said looking back at her before he closed the door behind him.

2320: Levi, Mueller and Morton headed for their squad cars.

"Have you got everything, Mueller?" Levi asked as he approached his squad car.

"Morton's got it all in the briefcase," Mueller said.

"I have to make a phone call and then I'll meet you by the bridge," Levi said out his car door window and quickly drove out of the parking lot. Three blocks down on State Street, he pulled to the curb and walked in the corner drug store. The cashier had her head down, thumbing through a magazine, never noticing him walking in. He headed for the phone booth.

Excitement mounting for what he was going to do, he smiled, dropped a dime in the slot, and dialed WB7-6932.

"Yes, hello?"

"Chief, this is Officer Levi Kanter. I was patrolling Grant Park when a man approached me stating he wanted to talk with you. He says he knows who the killer of those two businessmen is and where to find him. He won't tell me. He will only talk to you."

"At this hour? Kanter, it's after midnight! Bring him to my office in the morning, and I'll talk to him."

"Sir, he won't talk to anyone but you, and he won't wait long. If you want to know before that Detective O'Malley hears about this, you better come. You can make her look bad, and you and the department will shine in the eyes of the mayor and city council. You will get the credit for catching the killer and not O'Malley. It will be your picture on the cover of the newspaper and you giving a statement for the TV stations."

"Yeah, I see what you mean. Good thinking. It will look good at election time. I was in bed, Kanter, give me a good thirty minutes and I'll be there. He'll surely wait that long. Where should I go?"

"Meet me at the old warehouse on Clark Street. I'll keep him company until you get there."

"That place is condemned! Are you sure that's the place?" The chief questioned.

"Yes, it's a block from the rooming house where he lives."

"Alright, I'll be there." The chief hung up.

Levi grinned as he hung up and left, returning to his car.

Still standing in the police department's parking lot, Morton grabbed Mueller's arm.

"Please, let's don't do this. We could just go on our usual patrol and forget about Levi. If he asks, we just tell him we got called away."

"Shut up, Morton, and get your hand off me! You want everyone to hear you? Get in the car now!" Inside, Mueller continued. "Look, Levi has done this two other times and got away with it. There still aren't any clues or motives with either case, so stop worrying. The press has the story buried on page five. Levi went over this thoroughly. He knows what he is doing. It was a great idea to use the warehouse."

"If anyone is suspicious, this will throw them off. The lieutenant will be sending our shift officers up and down State Street, not these out of the way streets. The chief will be dealing with the mayor and the press. What we are doing and where we are will be the last thing on his mind."

"I can't stand another one. I can't eat or sleep. I jump at every strange noise. I'm sick to my stomach now just thinking about what is going to happen. I don't want to do this! Stop the car, I'm going to be sick!" Mueller turned onto a side street and Morton barely made it out of the car before becoming violent sick.

After a few minutes, she returned to the car.

"Honey, we have no choice. Levi has us over a barrel. If we don't participate, he'll march right into the chief's office and show him the pictures he's got when he caught us in the park that night. If he squeals, our ass is grass! Yeah, he'll hang for murders, but we will be out of a job."

"I'm with you on that. I was thinking of leaving when this was all over. I can't stand to look at him, and I wish I had never listened to you. I feel so dirty. This was supposed to be a game and we weren't supposed to be involved in any crime. I can't shake the sight of him skinning those two men. One more is going to send me over the edge." Tears rolled down Morton's cheeks.

"I was, too, so don't feel alone. I want to go somewhere far away from this city and start something new. I'm tired of hiding our relationship. I want to put this whole thing behind me and start to live again like a human. I feel dirty too." Sergeant Mueller pulled onto Clark Street and stopped by the far end of the dock.

"There's Levi. Let's go over to him."

Morton started to get out and lost her grip on the briefcase which opened, spilling the contents on the pavement.

"I'm sorry. Nothing broke and no one saw it." Mueller looked at her and shook her head.

"Get a hold of yourself, Morton. You've done this twice before."

The two officers walked slowly over to Levi. Steve could see them from the across the street.

Mitch had a perfect view of all three from the maintenance lot.

"Who's coming? Who's the victim? You told us with the first two," Morton asked.

"You'll see real soon." They saw headlights now.

The car pulled in by the dock. The engine turned off and the chief got out of his car. Mueller and Morton were stunned! "It's the chief! He's the victim!" Mueller whispered. The chief looked around and walked toward Levi.

“Where’s this man you were talking about, Kanter? I don’t see anyone else.”

“He’s inside. He didn’t want to be seen.”

“What’s Morton and Mueller doing here?” The chief asked when he saw the two officers.

“They saw the man talking to me and waving his arms around. They came for back up, should there be trouble. Not the greatest area you know,” Levi said as they approached the dock door. He opened the door and shone his flashlight as the chief followed him in.

“Fine, let’s get this over with. I’d like to get some sleep,” the chief grumbled.

When the four of them were inside, Levi closed the door and led the chief toward the chamber with a low light hanging overhead.

“Well, Klaus, you apparently don’t remember me.”

“What the hell are you talking about and why did you call me Klaus?”

“Why, Chief, that’s your real name. Klaus Kratz. Nazi officer in Auschwitz.”

“You son of a bitch! You don’t know what you are talking about! How dare you call me a Nazi!”

“Klaus, I’ll start at the beginning. You were our guard at building number eight. Remember that? Remember how we begged to use a bathroom but you let us live in our soiled pants and sleep in bunks that had the odor of urine in the straw. And only one thin blanket to cover part of us when it was way below freezing?”

“Oh, come on now. How could you forget? I haven’t! Not one day, not one night have I forgotten. And you never questioned what happened to some of the little boys. You know, the ones that froze to death in their beds. You gave us orders to move bricks for days in the freezing wind. When our hands were bloody, you wouldn't get us gloves."

"Kanter, what the hell are you talk…" The chief broke in.

"And when you were transferred to the men's building. There you tortured men that could hardly stand up." Levi continued pacing back and forth as he yelled at the chief. "You laughed that hideous laugh of yours after you kicked them when they couldn't stand up. When they were of no use to you and the other guards, you shot them and pushed them into trenches, they had made themselves, and set them on fire! They had dug their own graves! There's no way you have forgotten."

"I'll kill you for this, Kanter. You are full of shit!"

"And oh, Chief—excuse me—Klaus. What about the skinning of the Jewish men while some were still alive? Huh? I can't hear you! Speak up!"

Seeing the tension build, Steven and Mitch entered the warehouse. Mitch put his index finger to his mouth indicating to be quiet. Both remained in the shadows. Samantha eased out from between the gas cylinders and joined the two men a few feet from her.

"What the hell is going on here? I'm getting out of here!" The chief turned around and all but ran into Mitch.

"What are you doing here, Gillini? O'Malley, you too?"

"Yeah, Chief. We want to hear your story," Samantha responded.

"Hey, O'Malley?" Levi stepped away from the light and shone his flashlight on Samantha's face. "How did you two get in here?"

"Go on…you two…continue. I want to hear the rest of the story," Samantha said looking at Levi.

"This has nothing to do with you, O'Malley! Get back and stay out of it," Levi said.

Suddenly, Sgt. Mueller pushed Steve aside and went up to Samantha. "Detective O'Malley, Morton and I know nothing about this. Levi just told us to come with him tonight."

"Too late for lies, Sergeant. You rank over Levi. If you didn't know what he was planning, you would have asked. If he wouldn't say, you would have changed his mind in a heartbeat. You knew it wasn't a surprise birthday party for someone."

"I swear, O'Malley, we didn't know anything about this. Only heard stuff from other officers. Levi said it was just a game. He just wanted to scare both Miller and Kramer. He said it was just a game!" Mueller pleaded.

"What are you talking about, Mueller? Kanter, what is she talking about?" The chief asked, clearly not knowing what was going on.

"Chief, didn't you know Miller and Kramer were doctors in Auschwitz? Of course, you did. Both were involved in killing Jews in agonizing ways. I saw all three of you yank teeth with gold in them from the mouths of dead Jews. I saw all three of you force men to dig deep trenches that became their own graves."

"All three of you were ranked Nazi officers. Miller and Kramer escaped like you did just before the Russians liberated us. Kramer and Miller, both, ran businesses on Michigan Avenue and you…you became the all-powerful leader of the Chicago Police Department! The symbol of law and order. The leader of safety for the people of Chicago. How can you live with yourself?"

"Kanter, have you lost your mind?" The chief asked, raising his voice as he stepped back from Levi. "Where did you get this information? I'm trying to cut you some slack here. You need help. You're confused. I can get you help if you let me. The department will pay for any treatment that is required. You are and have been a good officer."

"You can be again. You just need some therapy and maybe some time off. I can arrange all of that for you. In the meantime, you can be off duty with pay until we find a good place for you," the chief said in a nervous voice.

"I've been going to a therapist for over a year, Chief. I've told him what I have lived with for all the years since liberation. All the horrible memories, the nightmares, the waking up screaming loud enough to have the neighbors in adjacent apartments knock on my door to see what is going on. I've told him how bad my head hurts to remember the things I've seen you and others do to Jewish people, to those with mental problems, and the gypsies."

"What you made them do. Thirty-some years to find all of you and, by God, I did! And the rest of the time, I dreamed of what I was going to do to make you go through the worse thing I could think of. So, I built this gas chamber like the ones in Auschwitz. You are going to be the first. I made it just like the one you forced men, women, and children to go into."

"Miller and Kramer were my test subjects. I wanted to be sure I could do it and get away with it. Mueller and Morton came along to help. I was saving the worst for you. I have the gas installed in the pipeline now. I made this just for you. You will be able to experience what those innocent people experienced."

"And I'm going to stand guard and make sure you get to the crematorium too. Just like you, Officer Kratz. Just like you did for days on end until thousands had been gassed and burned. I can still smell the odor that came out of the smokestacks. But I will enjoy smelling the odor from your smoking corpse. And I hope you end up in the darkest corner of Hell!"

"Where do you fit in, Mueller? Were you there too?" The chief asked.

"I wasn't born yet. I and Morton were made to go along with it or Levi was going to tell you of our secret," Mueller explained.

No sooner said than Morton walked out of the shadows and stood beside the chief.

"Get out of the way, Morton, this is between Kanter and me," the chief said, shoving Officer Morton away from him.

"What will it take for you to forget about this? Money? I can advance your rank. What do you need to put this behind both of us?"

"Oh, I will tell you in due time. I want to continue with your résumé while you were my guard in the death camp. You were promoted to one of the doctor's assistants in the hospitals. When I turned eleven, I was transferred to the building with older boys and had to work in both hospitals. The regular one that treated everyone and the women's hospital that cared for women about to give birth."

"We worked twelve-hour shifts. Remember that? We had to carry buckets and pick up body parts that weren't used in the experiments by Dr. Mengele and Dr. Miller…oh yes, I know what Doctor Miller's specialty was. I saw you strap teenage boys down while Miller castrated them. You were holding the pain medicine above them as they begged for it."

"You just laughed and laughed until they passed out. I know all of it! I've been reliving it all these years, you heartless animal."

"I don't have to stand here and listen to these lies and made-up stories. You are a sick man, Kanter." Chief Van Watson started to move closer to Levi when Mitch stepped forward. Levi went to the side of the chief and continued his rampage.

"Come over here, Chief. Look at the wall." Levi led the chief within inches of the pictures he had tacked to the chamber wall. "See these pictures? This is your life, Klaus Kratz. Remember that T.V. show? Only this is going to have a different ending. There won't be applause from the audience."

"Look at the pictures. That's my parents. This one is me and that's me starving to death. Here's another one of you. And here you are shooting an unarmed man."

"Levi, I want you in my office first thing in the morning. We will continue this in my office," the chief said avoiding looking at the pictures.

"Like hell we will. It's going to be settled here and now."

"Kanter, I'm your superior officer, and if you don't show some respect, I will bring charges against you! You are way out of line with this charade and I've had enough. I understand you are Jewish and a Holocaust survivor. I understand you have horrible dreams and the memories are hard to live with, but you are wrong about me."

"I've lived here all my life. Law enforcement has been a lifelong dream. Look at me, Kanter, I'm the chief! And my name is William Van Watson."

"You egotistical son of a bitch. I know everything about you. I have the documents showing when you changed your name. I have documents on Miller and Kramer too. They are in my car. I've watched you ever since I joined the department. I heard you laugh one time and knew I had heard it before. It took a long time to figure out where, and then it came to me."

"I remember when I saw you take the skin off my father. He was laying outside on a gurney in freezing temperatures, and you gave him no pain medication. I watched you take your knife out and remove the skin on his chest with him screaming in pain and you just stood there over him and laughed! That's what you did! Laugh! And you call me sick."

Samantha walked up between Mitch and Steve and faced Levi. "Levi, we know everything. All three of us. We know about the boots you removed from the evidence room. You gave them to Mrs. Kramer, didn't you? We had your car towed and the documents removed from the trunk. We were granted a search warrant to search your apartment and the Kramer's home."

"Do you know why I took them, O'Malley? I'll bet Kratz, here, has a pair of the same kind of boots in his home. How 'bout it, Kratz? Do you have a pair of boots with an area cut out in the heel that holds a cyanide pill? I'll bet you do. You escaped wearing them, didn't you?" Levi continued to drill the chief about the boots.

"I'm going to leave, Kanter. I've had enough of this charade." The chief turned away but Levi grabbed his shoulder and turned the chief to face him.

"Tell me what you did to my mother when Dr. Mengele was done with her. Tell me! I want to hear it from you!"

"*Ich bin unschuldig*," the chief yelled.

"You messed up, Chief! I understand German! You are not innocent! You just spoke in your native language! You put a bag over her head and let her suffocate to death! I saw this. All of it."

"I did what I was ordered to do. I had to do what I was told to do," the chief cried out.

"But you enjoyed it, Chief. You hated Jews. You enjoyed treating them worse than you would treat a dog. I want you to rot in hell for what you did."

"Okay. Okay. Let me explain." The chief's forehead was dripping with sweat now. "I had to get out of there. I would have been tried and probably hung. I only did what I was told to do by Himmler and the doctor. They were two men you didn't cross or argue with."

"I'm a decent man now, Kanter. I live a respectable life and do my job well. I can't undo what I've done and what other officers have done. It's history, and I have forgotten about my past."

"So easy for you, hasn't it been? Nazis don't have a conscious and can forget about what they did to six million innocent people. I'll bet you still attend Nazi meetings, don't you? I happen to know where you go on Sunday afternoons. You attend meetings on the south side of Chicago. Frank Collins is your leader."

"You were a co-sponsor in planning that assembly in Skokie a while back. The plan failed due to the large population of Jewish Holocaust survivors. Yes, you finally won the right to assemble in Marquette Park. Your feelings were that if seeing Nazis offended some people, then they should stay away."

"You didn't care in Skokie, and you don't care here about the emotional damage this causes seeing men in Nazi uniforms and Nazi insignias on arm bands. Chief, you still have a strong hatred for Jewish people. How many officers do you have in your department that are Jewish? You don't know, do you? Have you any idea what ethnic background your secretary is from? Of course not. Well, she is Jewish!"

"There are several Jewish officers on the force, and when they find out just what you are, you can bet the police force will be much smaller. I intend to see that happen." Levi pulled out his gun, dropped it to his side, and moved closer to the chief.

Samantha walked closer to Levi. "Levi, we will handle this issue in the proper way. The chief will be charged with war crimes just as the Nazi leaders were. We want you to win your case but we must do it right. Put the gun down and we will take the chief into custody. Levi, I'm on your side, but I'm going by the book on this one," Samantha spoke softly to him in hopes of calming him down.

She took a few more steps toward him and reached for his gun.

“No, O’Malley!” Levi turned and pointed the gun at Samantha. Mitch brought his weapon up and pointed it straight at Levi’s head. Samantha held her hand up to Mitch.

“Lower your gun, Mitch. Levi and I are just talking. I want to give him all the time he needs to vent. Learning about the chief is troubling, and we all want justice, but it must come in the right way.” Mitch lowered his weapon but remained in shooting stance.

Steve Jordon had angled himself to the side of the chief while Levi’s head was turned toward Samantha. He had seen the bulge under the chief’s left shoulder of his jacket and was watching the chief’s right hand. There had been moments that he made a visible fist.

“This is mine and mine alone,” Levi said. “The pain is too deep and the memories still too fresh to go the proper route. You heard him. He still hates Jews and still advocates the Nazi principles. I do this for all those who perished and those that survived, not just me. My belief is an eye for an eye. I want him to suffer in the same fashion as so many did. My parents for instance. My mother endured suffering for almost three years.”

Levi paused as if thinking…then continued. “As for the other issue, how did you know? Who told you, O’Malley, about tonight and meeting here?”

“I did! I told her everything including the plan tonight. I couldn’t stand another scene like the two before. You’re sick, Levi, and this wasn’t going to stop with tonight. You said yourself that if it took your entire lifetime, you would hunt down everyone that wasn’t caught. It makes me sick, Levi. My life is a wreck now. Sergeant Mueller and I will pay for what you have done,” Morton said angrily.

"Is this true? All three of you are involved in this?" The chief seemed surprised.

"Yes, we have been all along, Chief. It was supposed to be a game, Sir. Just to scare Miller and Kramer and let them know that Levi knew who they were. There was no mention of killing anyone. Neither Miller nor Kramer would have told the police because they would have to admit what and who they were. Miller and Kramer never saw our faces," Morton continued.

"She's right," Mueller butted in. "I'm sorry, Chief, but Levi threatened to tell you about Morton and me. What choice did we have? We both knew the department's policy on homosexuals. If you knew, then we would be out. Looks like we will be anyway." Mueller took a step closer to Levi. "We are all going to die for what you started, Levi. Right now, I don't care. I want it over."

"Get your hands up, Sergeant, and step away from Levi," Samantha ordered.

Suddenly, Morton started crying. "O'Malley knows everything. I told her. We were with Levi for the other two killings. Levi told us it was a game, there would be no killing. So, he got us to go along with the game, except there was killing and now we will hang too!"

Samantha walked over to Morton, unsnapped the holster, took her gun, removed the bullets, and handed it to Mitch. "Go stand next to Mueller, Morton, and keep quiet. We know everything. You don't have to say anything more."

The chief looked into Levi's eyes. "Levi, I swear I'm going to kill you. It will be in self-defense. You drew on me first, and I will tell the court that I said all those things thinking it would bid me time to think what to do. I may not get out of this alive but you will be dead and maybe O'Malley too. I'm not going to hang like the others."

Steve saw the chief raise his right hand and grab for his gun from the shoulder harness. Steve drew his gun and shot the chief in the leg. Levi screamed, "No, no! He's mine!" He raised his gun toward Steve. Mitch shot Levi in the arm as the chief faced Mitch. Just then, Steve fired and caught the chief in chest. The chief doubled over and fell to the floor. Levi turned and faced Samantha. He pointed his gun straight at her.

"This is all your fault, O'Malley. I put that note put in your newspaper several months ago to get you to drop your interest in the spilled chemicals at the warehouse, but no, you couldn't leave it alone, and now look where we are. The way things are now is your fault. It would have been cut and dry had you not interfered!"

Levi took two breaths and raised his injured arm and was about to shoot Samantha when she fired her gun from the pocket of her coat. Levi looked shocked as he clutched his chest and slowly went down on his knees. The chief brought his gun out of the shoulder holster when Steve said, "Don't do it, Chief. Put it down!"

"Why? It's all over, and I'll be damned if I stand trial."

At that moment, a blast of gun fire from Mitch and Steve left the chief sprawled on the floor in a pool of blood. Steve walked up and kicked the gun away from the chief's hand and checked for a pulse. He was dead. Mitch went to Samantha who had called for an ambulance and was bent down over Levi.

"You didn't win this way, Levi. I'm sorry," Samantha said in a low voice.

"He was mine. That's how I wanted it to end." A smile crossed Levi's mouth as he looked at Samantha. He coughed and gagged. "I had nothing against you until this. I wish you had stayed out of it. Damn, you're a better shot than I thought you would be." Levi tried to laugh and stared at the ceiling.

"It's over. I can sleep now. My head won't hurt and no more dreams. I'm free…I'm finally free." A small smile came over his face. He coughed and closed his eyes.

Steve Jordon cuffed Mueller and Morton and walked to the door. He took a long look back at Samantha. Mitch was there with her. They both were standing looking at each other. She had who she needed with her. He got in the squad car and headed toward the police department as two police cars with sirens blaring pulled into the parking lot.

Mitch helped Samantha stand and put his arm around her. "Are you okay?"

"Yeah, I think so. There are no winners here, is there? I had hoped it wouldn't end like this. Levi did some awful things but I had no idea about the chief." Samantha leaned against Mitch and looked down at Levi. "Mitch, you know that saying…freedom comes with a price?"

"Yeah, what about it?"

"Will we ever understand just how fragile freedom is?"

Mitch guided her away from the scene. "Let me take you home. Pretty sure someone there is anxious to see that you are all right."

THE END

Made in the USA
Monee, IL
24 May 2024